We appreciate our mega-amazing readers!

Sloane G., Maddy H., Dinah H., Christine D.-H., Olive Jean D., Eli Reuben D., Camren N., Zellah C., Callista P., Nadia H., Melody S., Maddilyn R., Zoey R., Brady R., Lucia P., Kali F., Eleanor A., the Andrade family, Kati B., Eleni P., Sabrina P., Lori F., Sabrina B., Natalie B., Lillia L., Kira L., Christina L., McKenna W., Lana W., Sarah M., Layla S., Sairi M., Lenny G., Kyla T., Adrian M., Neil T., Andy H., Paul H., Kristen S., George H., Barbara E., and you!

—J.H. and S.W.

CONTENTS

Prologue

MELINOE PLOPPED HERSELF TO SIT IN A CHAIR across a small table from Cassandra the fortune-teller. Cassandra stared at her in surprise, as many people did when they first met her. Because not only was Melinoe's skin pale and white—it glowed! And her long hair was black on one side of her head and white on the other.

"Name's Melinoe. And I've come with a question.

It's rumored that Zeus will one day name someone as the official goddessgirl of ghosts. I know I deserve the title. But will that King of the Gods ever make it happen? What can you tell me?" She set her hand, palm upward, onto the table.

"I will tell you what I see," Cassandra replied. Then she asked, "Um, you're a daemon, correct?"

Melinoe raised her chin and nodded haughtily. Daemons were immortal and had magic powers, though none as strong as those of a goddess. Still, she figured the powers she did have made her superior to this mortal girl, whose only talents were prophecy and cookie-baking.

"Okay, then." Cassandra bent forward to study Melinoe's palm. As Melinoe anxiously awaited her prophecy, she studied the fortune-teller's fire-gold hair and brown almond-shaped eyes. She guessed they were both about the same age—twelve.

To kill time, Melinoe gazed around the shop they were in. It was called Oracle-O Bakery and Scrollbooks and sold delicious treats as well as scrollbooks. Maybe she'd buy something on her way out to celebrate the good news Cassandra was about to tell her. Maybe.

Desperate to know if she would ever become a goddess, Melinoe had sought this girl out here, in her family's shop. It was located in the Immortal Marketplace, which stood halfway between Mount Olympus and Earth. The IM was enormous, with a high-ceilinged crystal roof. Rows and rows of columns separated the various shops, which sold everything from the newest Greek fashions to tridents.

She narrowed her eyes at Cassandra. Did telling

a fortune really take this long? It had been all of one minute already!

"Ah," Cassandra said at last. She flicked Melinoe a look. Not a hopeful one. Melinoe stiffened. She could tell from the girl's sympathetic expression that it was going to be bad news.

Cassandra hesitantly revealed her fortune. "You will get your wish. You will become goddessgirl of ghosts."

Huh? But that was *good* news. For several seconds joy filled Melinoe. But then uncertainty flooded over her, like a bucket of cold water. Because it was rumored that Cassandra was cursed in a way that made her foretell the opposite of what was true. So if she said you were going to turn into a pickle, that meant you would *not* turn into a pickle. For that reason, the fortunes Cassandra told were always placed inside special fortune cookies called Opposite Oracle-Os.

"Wait," said Melinoe. "Are you telling me the *opposite* of what will happen? Or what you think really *will* happen?"

Cassandra sighed. "The opposite. I'm sorry."

Furious, Melinoe yanked her hand from Cassandra's. She slammed her fist on the tabletop, making a plate of cookies in the middle jump. "If not me, then who will be chosen goddessgirl of ghosts? Tell me her name!"

"The goddessgirl of ghosts will not have stronger powers than you. And she will not be named Hecate," Cassandra told her.

"In other words she *will* have stronger powers than me, and *will* be named Hecate," fumed Melinoe. She leaped out of her chair. "So I will always be second best, is what you're saying." Reading the truth in Cassandra's eyes, a dark swirl of jealousy filled Melinoe.

“Here, have some free cookies. They’ll make you feel better.” Cassandra rose from her chair, grabbed a bag, and quickly filled it with the cookies from the plate.

“Wow, thanks!” Melinoe grabbed the bag, threw it to the floor, and crushed it under the heel of her sandal. “Oops! Sorry.” Then she sent Cassandra a sarcastic grin. “Not!”

Whipping around in a whirl of black-and-white hair, Melinoe called out, “Come!”

Unseen by anyone but her, a troop of pale white ghosts obeyed. All were animals. Gliding out through the shop’s walls, they followed her into the Marketplace.

There, she muttered a vow. “Better watch out, Hecate. I will find you! And when I do . . . You. Are. Toast!”

1

Flying Broom

AS HER TEACHER AND FELLOW WITCH-GIRL classmates watched, Hecate cautiously approached a magic broomstick. It hovered horizontally several feet above the ground, about five yards away, waiting for her. She was one of a very few in her grade who couldn't yet fly. Which was embarrassing! Especially since tomorrow was her birthday and she'd be turning twelve. By that age most girls had been flying for a year or two! But maybe today was the day she'd finally win her own broom.

Like the other witches here at Hexwitch School, the dark-eyed Hecate wore the standard uniform: a black chiton—which was basically a simple, flowy dress—plus red-and-white striped leggings and ankle boots. And, of course, a pointy black hat. Beneath it, her hair was long, black, and a little messy. She rarely combed it. Witches weren't supposed to have tidy hair!

Eyeing the broom, Hecate lifted a hand to fiddle with the necklace she wore—one she'd made herself. She possessed many such necklaces, each strung with small, square pieces of papyrus. Upon each piece she'd written one interesting fact she'd collected about a particular subject.

The facts on this necklace were all about brooms. She muttered one of them now to calm herself. "Witch brooms are made from grass, straw, hay, corn husks, or thin sticks that are tied onto a tree branch as a handle."

For some reason, learning and speaking random information made her feel more in control, and calmed her fears about the possibility of any bad stuff happening. Hexwitch School was located on Earth. And that could be a scary place. The day she'd turned six years old, for example, she'd been chased up a tree by a dog!

And that was only the beginning of her troubles with animals. Over the years she'd been scratched by a cat, nibbled by a rabbit, and pounced on by a squirrel. And a raccoon had once stolen her lunch right off the bench where she'd sat eating it! It was like she was like an animal-trouble magnet or something. If she could win her own broom today, she'd be able to make quick getaways from annoying animals and maybe other kinds of trouble too.

At last, Hecate stood next to the waiting broom.

"Hecate, meet Twitchy," her teacher Ms. Zoomly told her, gesturing toward the broom. It had a long black handle with dry brown corn husks tied at one end as the sweeping part.

"Hi, Twitchy," Hecate squeaked nervously. Her past failures at flying were weighing her down.

"Twitchy, meet Hecate," Ms. Zoomly told the broom.

It jerked and rattled its husks in reply.

"Remember, a witch needs to bond with her

broom," Ms. Zoomly reminded Hecate in a kind but firm voice. "You are not its boss and it is not yours. You'll act as partners. For flying to go well, you must respect one another."

Still feeling anxious, Hecate nodded. She'd heard this before. After all, this was her *twelfth* attempt at flying, each time with a different broom. If she wanted to avoid failing Broomstick Studies, she really needed to step it up.

Straightening, she pulled her hat's drawstring tight under her chin, so it wouldn't blow off once she was airborne. Her hand shook as she wrapped her fingers around the broom's shaft ten inches from the tip, as she'd been taught. Her teeth started to chatter. Her knees wobbled.

"If at first you don't succeed, try, try again," she

whispered. She'd read that somewhere. She only wished she knew how *many* times she'd have to try, though.

Quickly, she slung one leg over the broom's shaft. "Fly!" she commanded. Within seconds the broom took her soaring above the treetops. She'd launched before, but this was the first time she'd managed to get this high. So far, so good!

"You can do it!" "Go, Hecate!" she heard her classmates cheer from below.

She had only five minutes to complete her course. The goal was to fly in the shape of a pentagram, a five-pointed star that was the school symbol. It was embroidered on their school uniforms and on the school flag. Each point stood for a quality they were to strive for: kindness, responsibility, diligence, confidence, and honesty.

Hecate grinned as she and her broom successfully made the first point. And the second. Head down, she leaned left, indicating to the broom which direction to fly to make the next one. The wind cooled her cheeks and blew her hair into even more of a tangle as they turned. She hit the next point, no problem! She'd never made it to three points before. *Woo-hoo!* What a thrill! But the thrill didn't last.

Without thinking, she loosened her grip on the broom instead of guiding it into the next turn. Sensing her lack of control, it decided to misbehave. (Witch brooms were mischievous like that.) It darted left, then jerked right, then backward and forward again. It was like a wild horse trying to buck her off its back!

Somehow she managed to hang on. But then the broom flipped her upside down. It headed for a huge oak tree. They were going to crash!

Hecate unclasped her hands and knees from the sides of the broom. And suddenly she was falling! A haystack magically appeared on the ground below her, thanks to Ms. Zoomly. Teachers always took care to give students a soft landing.

Oof! She dropped on the hay, landing faceup. As she lay there, she watched Twitchy zip safely around the tree. Not crashing. Never even touching it. It curled its corn husks into a smile shape and wiggled merrily. It was laughing at her!

"That did not go well," she muttered. What if that wacky broom *had* crashed her into that tree? That was a scary thought.

"You'll do better next time," Ms. Zoomly told her encouragingly, while giving her a hand up from the hay.

Hecate stood and straightened her pointed hat,

loosening its drawstring. Her green-haired best friend, Willow, ran over and gave her a hug. "You did great!"

Her other best friend, Hazel, clapped. "Yeah, three points this time!" She was wearing hazelnuts as earrings.

"What's the opposite of nailed it?" said a third classmate, with bright orange hair. "Oh, yeah—*failed it.*"

Ugh. That mean girl was named Jinx.

Jinx's BFF, Agatha, smirked and added, "Again."

"Mm-hm," said Hecate. She managed a smile as she got to her feet and brushed the straw off her chiton. Jinx was supercompetitive. She seemed to think that the more other students failed, the better it made witches like her look when they succeeded. Wrong!

But Jinx was right about one thing. Hecate *had* failed again.

Whoosh! Overhead, a flock of broom-riding Hexwitch students zoomed by, ruffling the hair and chitons of everyone below. It was the school's Broom Zoom team, out practicing. They performed at sports and school events, flying in formation and doing tricks and fancy maneuvers.

As everyone watched, the team did the Wedding Cake, a formation with a row of nine flyers at its base, then eight, then seven, tapering up to only two at the very top. Then came the Leapfrog maneuver, which had them flying in horizontal lines while they leaped over one another.

If only Hecate could ever get good enough to make the team. Ha! Like that was going to happen. She couldn't even fly a broom for five minutes without falling off!

Still, she got lots more thumbs-ups and encour-

aging words from other students at dinner later that evening. "You'll do it next time," they told her.

Jinx and a few of her witch-girl followers cackled and stared, obviously relishing Hecate's failure. That stung a little. But she told herself not to worry about them. It helped to remind herself that she was better in Charmed Arts class than most girls at Hexwitch. Everyone had their strengths, right?

After dinner, Hecate dashed up the thirteen-story spiral staircase to her dorm room. (Thirteen was every witch's lucky number.) She was in a hurry. Because school still wasn't over. Her Creative Spelling class was going on a field trip tonight—to a cemetery!

In her room, a wind chime of metallic witch figures tinkled at her open window, which was framed by spiderweb-patterned curtains. She squeezed out

some black licorice-flavored toothpaste and then brushed her teeth. Next, she reached into her closet and grabbed one additional fact necklace, looping it around her neck. This one was strung with papyrus squares that contained facts about cemeteries!

All the girls had identical rooms with a four-poster bed, a small dresser, a desk and chair, two shelves, one closet, and a cozy stone fireplace. In Hecate's room, unlit wax candles of many sizes and shapes, which she'd made in Charmed Arts, sat all around.

Hecate grabbed a blue-and-topaz-colored candle. She'd mixed various herbs into its wax when she'd made it. Then she'd carved it with special symbols and infused it with glitter.

Once lit, different-colored candles could help you achieve specific magical purposes. Some colors could bring love or money. But blue brought protec-

tion, and topaz lent self-confidence. Two things she could have used during her broom test. Too bad it was considered a fire hazard to carry a candle while flying!

While holding on to the blue-and-topaz candle, she quickly spoke an incantation:

"Candle, candle, please alight,
To guide me safely through this night."

Pzzt! Instantly, the candle lit itself.

"Darkness has fallen! Come along, those of you in my Creative Spelling class!" she heard her teacher call up the stairs from below.

Hecate scurried over, snatched up a piece of charcoal from her unlit stone fireplace, and stowed it in her pocket. Then she grabbed a half dozen large

sheets of papyrus from her desk, rolled them up, tucked them in her bag, and slung its straps over one shoulder. After taking a calming breath, she grabbed her candle and dashed out of her room.

2

Creepy

HECATE AND THE REST OF THE WITCHES IN her Creative Spelling class met their teacher outside the Hexwitch School entrance. Each held supplies and candles. Once all twenty of them had gathered, the green-haired Ms. Frogwart led them off to the cemetery.

Ms. Frogwart was one of her favorite teachers.

Hecate had even tried several times to cast a spell on herself to grow a cool wart on her chin to match the one her teacher had. But so far she'd been no more successful at this than at flying. Given her anxious nature, Hecate figured the only wart she might ever grow was a *worry*wart!

When they stepped into the cemetery through a huge iron gate, Ms. Frogwart surveyed the students. "Everyone bring their supplies?" she asked. After they all nodded, she went on, lighting the candles of each student. "You're here to make gravestone rubbings using your charcoal and papyrus. These rubbings will serve as inspiration for new magic spells you'll create in class over the coming days."

As the teacher spoke, Hecate gazed around the cemetery. It was surrounded by an elaborate wrought-iron fence decorated with silhouettes of fantastical flowers and animals. According to a nearby sign, the cemetery was divided into numerous labeled sections.

"A reminder," Ms. Frogwart went on. "We've gotten special permission to come here tonight to make our rubbings. But please be respectful of the dead. Do not run wild. Do not damage the gravestones. This is an old cemetery, and some of them may be fragile. Now, off with you!"

So saying, the teacher seated herself on a stone bench near the entrance gate to wait for their return in one hour. She pulled out a knitting project from the handbag she carried: long red-and-white leggings, from the look of it. Witches could never have too many pairs of those!

As the students headed off, Ms. Frogwart looked up from her knitting to call out, "One last thing. Do not get separated. A full moon is rising, and there may be ghosts or tricksters lurking."

Oh, great, Hecate thought with a shiver. *Something else to worry about.* Following the group, she drifted her fingertips over the necklaces she wore as they all went in search of gravestones carved with clever sayings or intriguing art. Moonlight and their candles lit the way.

On all sides of the path they spotted upright gravestones made of granite, marble, and bronze. There were also grave slabs lying flat on the ground, and tall, fancy monuments. Flowerpots containing lilies or roses sat at many of the grave sites. Some had a bench nearby where she supposed visiting relatives might sit.

Hecate shivered when a spooky shadow passed over her. Cast by the lush ivy and trees that grew

all around, shadows were everywhere! Naturally, when spooked, she couldn't keep herself from spewing random facts. As quickly as they occurred to her, they sprang from her lips as she and her classmates roamed the cemetery.

"Hey, did you guys know that Romans came up with the idea of gravestones to mark a burial site?" she babbled. "Also, Egyptians used to put a dead person's liver and other organs inside sealed jars that they expected would journey with their owner into an afterlife. They believed the heart was what did a person's thinking, not their brain."

"Ew! You are *waaay* too weird," Jinx told her, making an *ick* face. Unfortunately, Hecate's best buds, Willow and Hazel, weren't in this class. But Jinx and her friend Agatha were.

Hecate grinned over at them. Trying to be

friendly and jokey, she said, "Is there really such a thing as *too* weird for a witch? I think not."

A freckle-faced girl, new to the school, grinned back. "Yeah, Hecate's just the right amount of weird." Hecate smiled at her. Because that was a nice thing to say!

"Why are you so obsessed with collecting facts anyway, Hecate?" Jinx scoffed. "You need a better hobby."

"Yeah, instead of spending all your time gathering facts, like some kind of know-it-all, maybe you should practice your broomstick skills," snickered Agatha.

Hecate hunched her shoulders, cringing. Because they were kind of right. It was hard to explain just why she needed her facts, without sounding *mega*-weird.

A light breeze blew in just then, rattling the ivy that crept along the ground and wound up tree trunks, and causing their candles to flicker. This cemetery was creepy at night.

Witches were not supposed to be scared of creepy stuff, of course. But Hecate couldn't help that she was. Knowing and speaking facts aloud really did soothe her anxiety. It was like the facts built an invisible fence around her that made her feel safer in scary situations.

Faster and faster, words fell from her lips as she began blabbing more facts: "A graveyard is often smaller than a cemetery. . . . Sayings on gravestones are called epitaphs."

She felt annoyed glances being cast her way. Glimpsed the rolling of eyes, even from a few witches who were usually friendly toward her. It was really too bad that not everyone enjoyed facts as much as she did!

Luckily, their attention soon shifted to the assignment. Students began to read aloud the sayings on gravestones as they made rubbings. Some were surprisingly funny.

"Hey, look at this one!" said the new girl. She pointed to a particular gravestone. Hecate read it aloud:

"SY KICK

I KNEW THIS WOULD HAPPEN."

She grinned at the new girl. "I guess Sy Kick was *psychic*!"

"Yeah," said the girl, giggling. "Looks like he predicted his own death."

"Here's another fun one," said Jinx. She read it aloud:

"O. SHUN SWIRLY

MY SHIP WAS NAMED POSEIDON.

WE SAILED THE GREAT BLUE SEA.

TILL (WHOOSH!) THERE CAME A TIDE IN.

THAT WAS THE END OF ME."

"Ha!" said Hecate. "Here's what I want my gravestone to say:

"HECATE WITCH

HER SCRAGGLY HAIR

AND DRESS WERE BLACK.

HER FINAL WORDS WERE:

'I'LL BE BACK!'"

Her classmates laughed at her silliness, even the mean ones.

"Would you want to come back as a ghost?" asked Jinx. Since witches weren't immortal like the goddesses and gods of Mount Olympus, they'd all die someday too, just like human mortals.

Hecate shuddered. *Ghosts, ugh.* Talk about scary!

She shrugged and tried to sound calm as she replied, “Who knows? Maybe I *will* come back as a ghost.” She held her hands up and wiggled her fingers. “So I can haunt *YOOOU*!”

Jinx’s eyes got scaredy-big for a second, but then she acted all cool. *Huh.* Maybe Hecate wasn’t the only one around here who was afraid of ghosts!

Just then, Hecate noticed a cool ivy design carved on a flat, rectangular grave slab a short distance away. She wandered over and set her candle on one corner of the slab. Then she got a sheet of papyrus out of her bag, unrolled it, and laid it over the ivy design.

Scritch-scratch. She carefully rubbed the charcoal she’d brought across the papyrus. Back and forth it went, until the ivy engraved along the outer edges of the gravestone showed up. Slowly she worked her way in toward the center of the stone, capturing both the words and patterns carved upon it with her charcoal.

Meanwhile, she chattered away to her classmates. “I can tell this is English ivy because it has five-pointed leaves and grows on a vine.” Although no one remarked on this, she went on rambling. “Did you know poison ivy is not really ivy? It’s related to pistachios and cashews. Poison ivy has three leaves. There’s a rhyme to help you know not to pick it. It goes like this: ‘Leaves of three, let it be.’”

Jinx, who was rubbing at a nearby monument, snorted. “Argh, would you stop with the random info, Wreck-AH-tee?”

Hecate frowned over at her. “Did you just try to give me a nickname? Because . . . uh . . . *no thanks*.”

“Well, you did almost have a wreck on your broom during fly-out today,” Agatha taunted.

"Show some respect," Hecate blustered. "After all, I'm named for . . . someone famous. My, um, grandmother. Yeah, that's it."

"Wait, you mean Ms. Hecate at MOA?" asked another classmate, sounding surprised. By MOA, she meant Mount Olympus Academy, the famous school that stood atop the highest mountain in Greece. Hecate had never been there, and no one else she knew had either. Its students were all goddessgirls and godboys, plus a few lucky mortals.

Jinx looked up from the rubbing she was making, her expression skeptical. "Ms. Hecate? The witch who teaches Spell-ology there? She's your grandmother?"

"Mm-hm," Hecate mumbled before she could stop herself. She'd hadn't been thinking of that teacher, actually, and only just now remembered there was such a person at MOA. Though they shared a name, they were not related.

Since Ms. Hecate was an MOA teacher, her powers and magical expertise were well-known and admired by all. Hecate liked that her classmates seemed impressed, yet she kind of regretted her lie. Still, she didn't know how to take it back without making everyone think less of her.

And, anyway, if there were ghosts and tricksters lurking around here tonight, they might've overheard. If they thought she was related to the powerful Ms. Hecate, maybe that knowledge would keep them away from her and her classmates. So her lie could actually do some good!

"C'mon, you guys," someone called. "We'd better keep working. We don't have all night here."

When the group of students moved down the path

in search of more interesting gravestones, the new girl with freckles caught up to walk beside Hecate. "I have a famous name too," she told Hecate. "Or more like infamous. It's Poinsettia."

"That's a really pretty flower," said Hecate. "But it can be poisonous. I mean if you eat it. No offense."

Poinsettia grinned at her. "That's okay. That's what I meant by infamous." They walked a bit farther; then she went on. "I didn't think Ms. Hecate was old enough to be a grandmother."

Hecate hesitated, then added, "Mmm . . . well, she is."

Jinx had been listening in, and now piped up. "If you truly are her granddaughter, wouldn't that make you a goddess like she is? Yet your skin doesn't shimmer like an immortal's."

Uh-oh. Hecate didn't actually have an answer for

that. That was the thing about lies. They led to more lies. And you had to keep them all straight. Should she just tell her classmates the truth and face the consequences? Yes, she should!

After taking a deep breath, she opened her mouth to admit she'd just been joking around before about Ms. Hecate. But right then someone blurted, "Hey, look at these awesome gravestones over here!"

All the witch-girls rushed over and crowded around to make rubbings of the highly decorated gravestones in that part of the cemetery. Except for the *scritch-scratch* of charcoal on papyrus, all was quiet as they got to work. To Hecate's relief, her (false) claim to fame seemed forgotten for now. And the moment for confessing had passed. So, as she began making another rubbing, it was easy to let her lie—er, *joke*—go uncorrected.

Once some of the students finished, Hecate heard them discussing which way they should all go next. They were at a crossroads. Directional signs indicated the various sections, but gave no description of what they'd find there.

While the others talked it over, Hecate spotted a gravestone decorated with an awesome winged hourglass carving. She pulled a fresh sheet of papyrus from her bag, dropped to her knees, and began making a rubbing of it. At the same time, she automatically murmured facts under her breath. "A winged hourglass is a symbol for the saying 'Time flies.' . . . Lamb etchings are sometimes carved on children's gravestones."

Eventually, she realized the others had stopped speaking. She carefully rolled up her papyrus, then stood, tucking it into her bag and pocketing her charcoal. Then she turned around to see that . . . her classmates were gone!

"Hey! You guys!" she shouted. No answer. "Where'd everybody go?" Still no answer. She was *alone*!

Making a guess as to where they might have gone, she turned down a path. Was she going the right direction? She hurried on, calling out to her classmates every few steps.

Eventually, a reply came back. *OO-ooo-ooo!*

A shiver ran down her back. That was *not* one of her classmates. It was the howl of a dog! A real dog? Or a ghostly one? Either would be terrifying!

Hecate took off running, up one path and down another. A few minutes later, she thought she heard a girl's voice. "Hello?" she called.

Following the sound, she pushed through a small

iron gate and then fought the long vines of ivy hanging just beyond it. All at once, she found herself in a new section of the cemetery. Here the grave markers were smaller, for some reason. Seeing a large stone sign at the end of the path, she sped toward it, then stilled, her heart pounding. Because upon it were carved two large words: PET CEMETERY.

"'Pet'?" Hecate whispered to herself in alarm. "As in *animals*? Oh nooo!"

3 Ghosts

But, yes, judging from the images of animals carved upon nearby gravestones, it appeared that Hecate had indeed entered a pet cemetery! Shivering now, she backed away from the sign, continuing to call for her classmates.

OO-ooo-ooo! answered the dog (or dog *ghost*). More animal sounds began to float in the air around her. *Caw! Meow! Squeak! OO-ooo-ooo!*

"It's okay. I'm okay," Hecate chanted to herself. Her gaze flew around the pet cemetery. Where, oh, where was that gate she'd opened when she'd accidentally entered it? It seemed to be hidden by the vines of ivy she'd pushed through. She began to feel her way along the nearest wall, hoping to uncover the gate.

She'd once memorized facts about what to have with you in case you ever got lost in the wilderness, and she purposely called them to mind now. "Always carry a map, compass, whistle, water, first aid kit, pocketknife, and light," she recited. She didn't have any of those! Well, except for her candle. So far, it hadn't blown out. That was something.

The wind picked up. She cupped her hand around her candle as she moved along another wall. Shadows loomed on all sides of her. The long woody vines of ivy reached out like bony fingers trying to grab her.

Suddenly, Hecate spotted a flash of white light in the darkness to her left. She crouched next to a moss-covered gravestone with a dog carved on it, watching for trouble. Quietly, she murmured an incantation, hoping to ward it off.

"Keep me safe from stones and sticks
And those who'd harm me with their tricks."

Had she said that right? Was "tricks" the correct word? Or was it "kicks" or "bricks"? Incantations wasn't her best class at Hexwitch. To be honest, with the exception of Charmed Arts, she wasn't doing that great in any of her classes.

The trouble was, she spent far too much time

gathering facts and thinking up ways to avoid possible disaster instead of studying. Over the years, more than one teacher had said things to her like *You're smart, Hecate. If you work harder and pay more attention to your lessons, and less attention to things that don't matter*—such as the facts she accumulated daily, they meant—*you'll do really well*.

As she was thinking this, a girl about her same age suddenly stepped in front of her. "Hi, Hecate. Enjoying this boo-tiful moonlit night?"

"Eek!" Hecate leaped up so abruptly that she dropped her candle. It landed upside down and was snuffed out. She stepped back, her eyes going wide. Because the girl was kind of . . . translucent! Her entire body glowed a pale white color. And her hair was black on one side of her head and white on the other side.

"Boo-tiful? You mean *beautiful*? And h-how d-do

you know my n-name?" Hecate was trembling all over, and her knees felt like buckling.

"I heard you and your friends talking earlier. I'm Melinoe." The girl took an eager step forward. "Have you heard of me?"

Hecate shuffled backward, her eyes darting around for an escape. "Um, no." Looking disappointed, Melinoe gave a little annoyed huff.

From the corner of her eye, Hecate kept seeing more strange flashes of white light. It must be fear causing her to imagine them. Right? But then some of them began to take shape. Sharp teeth. Big claws. Furry faces. No sooner did they come into focus than they were gone again.

Caw! Meow! Squeak! OO-ooo-ooo!

"Did you hear that?" she asked Melinoe.

"Hear what? *Ghostly* sounds, you mean?" The

glowing girl smiled a sneaky smile. She whirled in a circle, causing her gown to swirl around her. By the time she stopped, her skin glowed even more brightly. She dramatically raised her arms out to her sides. "Come out, come out, wherever you are," she called.

The white flashes Hecate had seen earlier began to form themselves into definite shapes. Then those shapes floated down from trees and passed right through gravestones, gathering closer and closer to her and Melinoe. As Hecate's gaze darted from one to another, her horror grew. The shapes were turning into . . . animals!

Some were everyday animals—a cat, a dog, and a pig. Animal noises began to fill the air. This was her worst nightmare come true!

"Go away!" she shrieked, shrinking back from

them. Appearing surprised and maybe a little hurt by her attitude, the animals stopped moving closer. Sorry, but they terrified her!

"Stop screeching! You'll scare them," Melinoe scolded her. Then, to all her animals, she said in a gentler voice, "It's okay, guys, you didn't do anything wrong. She's just a scaredy-witch." She bent and stroked a hand along the back of a dog.

Then Melinoe gasped, her chin jerking back in surprise as she straightened again to study Hecate. "Wait! You can see them? My ghost animals?"

Hecate nodded, eyes bugging out. "So you . . . and they . . . you're all g-g-ghosts?"

Melinoe waved an arm toward the animals. "*They're* ghosts. *I'm* not. I'm more of a ghost *herder*. At least that's what I call myself. I'm actually a daemon." She glared at Hecate as if that were somehow her

fault. And then Melinoe added haughtily, "I lead the ghosts of pets and other animals to the River Styx, so they can then cross it to reach the Underworld. It's not my official job. I do it out of the goodness of my heart. I'm excellent at it too."

She didn't sound good-hearted. She sounded angry and defensive. Like she saw Hecate as some kind of threat. But why?

"So you and your animals—you're all from the Underworld?" Hecate asked politely, hoping to calm Melinoe's strange anger. She lowered her voice to ask, "Do they bite?"

Melinoe put a hand on one hip. "Don't you know anything?" she scoffed. "No, they don't bite. They're *ghosts*. Which is a term for the dead that refuse to enter the Underworld. Like these stubborn critters." She gestured in the direction of the animals, which were now frolicking around with each other. "They're no longer alive, yet still linger here on Earth. If I can ever convince them to cross into the Underworld at last, they'll become *shades*. Dwelling in the Underworld would be so amazing; I don't understand why they wouldn't want to go there!"

Huh? The Underworld was a scary place; didn't this girl know that? thought Hecate. Various facts she'd collected indicated that it was located deep inside the Earth, and it was said to be gloomy and horrible. A godboy named Hades ruled it, and his large, three-headed dog, Cerberus, guarded its entrance.

"So is that why you came to the pet cemetery tonight?" Hecate angled her chin in the direction of the glowing white animals scampering around them. "To gather them and take them to the River Styx?"

"Maybe. But enough about them. Animals, be gone!" she ordered with a snap of her fingers.

To Hecate's relief, the animals instantly disappeared. She decided to take this opportunity to start sidling away. "Okay, I guess I'll just be going too. I'm here with my class. We're on an assignment. I better go catch up." She just wished she knew which way they'd gone!

Just then, Melinoe's gaze fell upon Hecate's necklaces. She stepped closer, appearing intrigued. "Awesome necklaces. What's written on those little squares of papyrus?" She flicked one of the squares with her fingertip.

Hecate reached up to clasp the necklace. "Nothing. Just, um, some facts I collect." She was actually kind of proud of the decorative lettering she used on her cards, but she rarely showed her artistry to anyone.

"Ah yes," said Melinoe. "I heard you talking with your friends over on the people side of the cemetery earlier. Your facts are so interesting."

"You think so?" Hecate asked. Brightening, she stopped trying to leave.

Melinoe nodded. "It's just too bad your friends didn't enjoy them."

Hecate slumped her shoulders. "You noticed that, huh?"

Melinoe nodded again, seemingly sympathetic. "I can tell that you really want them to appreciate your little hobby."

"That would be nice," said Hecate, giving a slight shrug.

"*Hmm.* I have an idea that might help," Melinoe offered after a few seconds. She smiled slowly. It was kind of an eerie smile, but Hecate didn't let on, since

the other girl was being supportive. "Maybe instead of just telling your friends facts, you could pose your facts as questions," Melinoe went on. "You know, offer them several choices of answers. Get them involved."

"You mean make it like a game?" Hecate asked, cocking her head to one side. "So they have to guess which of the answers is correct?"

"I hadn't exactly thought of it that way, but yes," said Melinoe. "A game. It would be more fun to guess answers than to just listen to facts, don't you think?"

"Yeah," said Hecate, quickly warming to the idea. "And suggesting three possible answers would help those who know the answer but can't recall it when put on the spot!"

"True," Melinoe agreed. "And if someone *doesn't* know the answer, there's still a chance they could accidentally guess it right."

Hecate nodded. Quickly she tore off a small blank square from one of the big sheets of papyrus she carried in her bag. She wrote on it with the charcoal she'd been using for rubbings.

"Like this, for example?" She read aloud what she'd written: "'Which Greek god carries a three-pronged pitchfork called a trident? Apollo, god of truth, prophecy, and music? Ares, god of war? Or Poseidon, god of the sea?'"

"Exactly!" Melinoe clapped her hands, grinning that strange smile of hers. "And the answer's Poseidon."

"Correct!" said Hecate, smiling back. Maybe this

girl wasn't so bad after all, in spite of her odd manner and her earlier angry tone.

"I've got another one," Hecate announced. She wrote it down before reading it aloud. "'What's the name of the black-and-white cat that the goddessgirls Aphrodite and Persephone share? Sweetie Pie, Newt, or Adonis?'"

"Not sure. I'm guessing Newt?" said Melinoe.

"Bzzt!" Hecate said, making a sound like a "wrong" buzzer. "Sorry, the answer to that one was Adonis."

"See? I just learned something and had fun doing it," said Melinoe. "Ooh! I thought of one. What's the food and drink of the gods? Toads and tea, flowers and nectar, or ambrosia and nectar?"

"Ambrosia and nectar!" said Hecate. "Hey, this is fun! But I'd better not always put the correct answer last. People would figure that out and always be

able to guess right. The game would be too easy." Before she could forget, she wrote that last Q&A (as in "question and answer") on a third square of papyrus, putting "ambrosia and nectar" as the middle answer this time.

"Let me write one. It won't be as nicely lettered as yours, but can I?" suggested Melinoe. When she held her hand out, Hecate gave her the piece of charcoal and a square of papyrus. She was pleased that Melinoe had noticed and appreciated her careful handwriting.

Melinoe began to write. *Snap!* "Oops! I broke your charcoal!"

"Oh! Too bad, because we were on a roll with these game facts," said Hecate in disappointment.

"No problem. I know a simple spell to fix it." Melinoe cupped the charcoal in both her hands, folding her fingers around it. Then, in a flurry of black-and-white hair, she whirled around, chanting.

Hecate couldn't make out all her words. They sounded to her like *magic, something something, bring, something something, fame, something something, name*.

Eventually Melinoe stopped chanting and whirling. She held out her hand to Hecate. In her palm was a whole, unbroken piece of charcoal!

"Wow! Thanks," said Hecate, taking it. "I don't know how to do a spell that changes something broken into something unbroken. It looks like new."

Melinoe twirled a finger in her hair and sent Hecate a sly look. "It's better than new, actually."

Hecate studied the charcoal closely. When she looked back up, Melinoe was gone. "Melinoe? Hey, where did you go?"

Hecate looked all around, but couldn't find her.

At that very moment, Melinoe was peeking out from a hiding place within the thick ivy that hung low to the ground from the branches of a nearby tree. Gleefully, she observed Hecate tucking the charcoal in her pocket. She'd set her plan in motion. Now she only had to wait for that plan to unfold.

Suddenly, a pack of ghost dogs howled spookily. Hecate let out a shriek of terror. Melinoe covered her mouth to keep from laughing and giving her hiding place away. She watched Hecate grab her bag and candle and finally manage to escape the pet cemetery.

Melinoe followed, darting from tree to tree and always remaining hidden. Eventually, Hecate found a sign that pointed her back to where her teacher and classmates awaited her at the entrance gate. The teacher frowned at Hecate when she joined them, causing the large wart on her chin to wiggle. However, she didn't scold, but simply gathered her with the other girls. Then they all headed back to Hexwitch School.

Melinoe wiggled her fingers in a small wave. “Good-bye, for now, Hecate,” she sing-songed quietly. But the look in her eye was one of jealousy.

Then, with a considerably fonder glance, she beckoned to the animals. “Come along, guys. Follow me in two rows, buddy system, so no one gets lost.” As she floated deeper into the pet cemetery, the ghost animals followed her. Melinoe didn’t notice as one pair scampered off the other way—to follow Hecate instead.

4 Cursed

BACK IN HER DORM ROOM THAT NIGHT, HECATE undressed, tossed her hat to rest atop a tall bedpost, and then put on her black-and-red polka-dot pj's. She was super-tired but, even so, couldn't fall asleep. For one thing, those ghosts in the pet cemetery had been terrifying!

Plus she was kind of excited about the new game idea Melinoe had suggested. Wide awake, she went to sit at her desk. There she wrote a whopping sixty game questions and answers on small pieces of papyrus. She had so many facts bottled up in her brain that more and more ideas just kept coming! She strung all the new question squares on one long necklace.

Eventually she found she couldn't stop yawning and finally headed for bed. She snuggled up in her blankets. Turning her head on her pillow, she caught a whiff of lavender, chamomile, and mugwort. She'd stuffed those and other herbs into a pouch, which she'd tucked inside her pillowcase. Together they created a comforting scent that was supposed to invoke good dreams. *Mmm.* It smelled sooo good.

Hecate was almost asleep when a flash of sparkles caused her eyes to spring open. *Hey!* She sat bolt upright, blinking at her arm. Was that glitter on her elbow? If so, it could be an indication she'd acquired a new magical power! Or a curse. *Hmm.*

She ran to the window to check the large moondial in the school courtyard far below. It was after midnight—officially her birthday. She was twelve now! And on a witch's birthday, magical changes could happen to her. However, the sparkles on her elbow rapidly disappeared. Must've only been some glitter from the candle she'd carried tonight, she decided. She hopped back in bed, curled up under her covers again, and fell fast asleep.

It seemed like she'd only just begun snoozing when she heard a songbird outside her window. It was morning. Hecate stretched both arms high and yawned. Then she opened her eyes and blinked in surprised alarm. Because Melinoe's ghost cat was sitting at the foot of her bed! Staring at her!

"*Agghh!*" she screamed.

Other witch-girls from her dorm rushed into her room. "G-ghost!" she shrieked, pointing.

"What? Where?" The girls looked all around.

"Right there," yelled Hecate, her finger pointed at the cat. "You can't see it?" Too frozen to actually leave her bed, she scrunched herself into a ball against the headboard. That put at least a little distance between her and the ghost cat.

"Nuh-uh," said Poinsettia.

"Weirdo," she heard Jinx mutter.

"Are you sure you aren't just still half awake and dreaming?" asked Hazel.

Hecate glanced from the ghost cat to her classmates, then shrugged. "Yeah, maybe." Obviously, this cat was invisible to them. They already doubted her supposed-grandmother tale from last night. If she told them what had happened in the cemetery, it seemed unlikely they'd believe her without some proof. And she *had* none. Jinx had already called her a weirdo. She couldn't risk others deciding that nickname was fitting!

Ding-a-ling! It was the breakfast bell. Everyone scrambled to go get dressed before heading down to the cafeteria. Once her classmates left, Hecate suddenly recalled how Melinoe had banished the animals in the cemetery.

"Cat, be gone!" Hecate commanded now. Unfortunately, the cat did not get gone. Instead it yawned at her, curling its pink tongue and displaying sharp teeth. She gasped. "Melinoe said you don't b-b-bite, right?" She figured it wouldn't understand her. But, to her surprise, it nodded calmly. It *had* understood! Well, good to know.

Still, as she got dressed, she kept a wary eye on it as she put on several of her fact necklaces. Once she'd grabbed her schoolbag and hat and was ready to go, she had an alarming thought. Was it safe to leave this cat alone in her room?

"Uh, ghost animals don't need litter boxes or food or water or anything, do they?" she asked it. The cat shook its head. That was a relief! She ducked around it and slammed the door behind her, shutting it inside her room.

"Eek!" Hecate shrieked when she reached the stairs. Not only had the cat magically appeared to sit on the top step, but there was now a ghost dog standing beside it!

"Sh-sh-shoo!" she commanded, flicking her fingers at them. The cat yawned again. The dog rolled onto its back as if wanting her to rub its tummy. *Um, no!*

"D-d-don't even think about following me," she told them. Then she zipped past them down the steps. But did they listen? Nope! They followed her.

Downstairs, the minute she entered the cafeteria, she spotted a cute sign newly hung on the wall. It was a big drawing of a cupcake that had a face, arms, and legs. It startled her when it chirped, "Happy birthday, Hecate!"

The drawing was magical! Friends—probably Willow and Hazel—must have made it. And they'd also cut cute footprints out of colored papyrus and laid them in a path from just inside the cafeteria door to a table loaded with dozens of cupcakes. A bunch of Hecate's classmates had gathered around, waiting for her!

"Those are for you," Willow told her. She pointed to the twelve especially fancy cupcakes on a black plate. “These are actually very nutritious. But we added magic to the frosting.”

“Yeah. So just tell the cupcakes whatever scrumptious flavor you desire and they’ll become that flavor,” Hazel added. Then she pulled out a chair with black and red balloons tied to its back and gestured for Hecate to sit.

“Wow! Thank you! You guys are the best,” said Hecate, giving her two friends hugs. Willow lit the twelve candles (one in each of the special cupcakes), and Hecate blew them out promptly and sat in the balloon-decorated chair. Classmates quickly filled the other chairs at her table to eat too.

“Ooh! Someone’s breath is *awful*!” said Jinx, who’d sat down beside her. She stared at Hecate accusingly, waving a hand to fan her face.

It wasn’t Hecate’s breath that was stinky. It was

the ghost dog's! It had come to sit on the floor between the two of them. Though none of these witches seemed able to hear or see the ghost animals, Jinx, at least, could smell the dog's breath. Hecate could too, unfortunately. *Pew!*

Abruptly, the ghost dog planted its front paws on the table and licked one of Hecate's special cupcakes before she could stop it. Then it ran off. *Ick!* Now the cupcake probably had yucky (but invisible) ghost-dog slobber on it. No way was she going to eat that one. Still, when she instructed half of the cupcakes to become vanilla, it still got included. She made the other half lemon and promptly ate two of those.

"Vanilla's my favorite," she heard Jinx say. "You don't mind, do you?" Without waiting for a reply, she stole the slobbered-on vanilla cupcake, shoved it into her mouth, and then smirked.

Hecate almost burst out laughing! She couldn't help chuckling as she put the rest of her cupcakes in a box, which she slid into her bag for later. Ha-ha! If Jinx only knew!

After breakfast, the pair of ghostly animals trailed Hecate to Incantations, her first-period class. There the cat sat on top of her desk and licked its paws, staring at her. The dog lay across her feet, keeping them warm. Although she was definitely not a fan of animals, that did feel kind of nice.

Today she and her classmates were instructed to practice casting simple, temporary spells on unsuspecting mortals. The various chants and hexes Ms. Wanda had taught them could be tried out long-distance on girls at the nearby Sensible Mortal School. Using the extra-large crystal ball that sat atop her desk, Ms. Wanda would be able to view and grade Hecate's spell-casting efforts and those of the other students. Usually these spells involved turning the mortal girls into newts or toads. Or giving them a bad hair day, burps, or hiccups, or maybe causing them to say something embarrassing.

Hecate had already mastered all those particular spells. Today she decided to try something new. A double spell, which she could plan and view while gazing into her smaller, student-size crystal ball. Peering into it now, she spotted a mortal girl tripping another girl and then laughing at her for being clumsy. Not cool. Quickly, Hecate came up with and spoke a spell.

"Mean girls deserve to get an itchy rash
And grow a wiggly, weird mustache!"

Her spell worked! In her crystal, she watched everyone around the mean girl begin pointing and laughing. Served her right. The rash and mustache Hecate had given her faded away before the girl could complain about it to a teacher.

"Nicely done," commented Poinsettia. She and Hazel had both leaned over to watch the scene unfolding inside Hecate's crystal ball.

"Thanks," said Hecate.

Hazel nodded. "Yeah! Mustaches aren't easy. That's a sure A grade."

Hecate smiled at them. It was nice that things were looking up, grade-wise, on her birthday. Not so nice that she had acquired two furry companions.

She had managed to ignore both the cat and the dog during Incantations. But when she walked through the halls on the way to second-period Charms class, the cat wound around her ankles in a figure eight. This tripped her up, making her do a silly little dance. The dog trotted behind her. No one but her appeared to hear the *click-click* of its toenails on the floor.

Strangely, there were times when the cat and dog seemed almost solid. She could often feel their warmth and sense the weight of their bodies, for example. And sometimes she could hear sounds they made, other times not. Still, if ghosts could pass through walls, why didn't they sink through floors when they walked? Who knew? Ghost magic must operate in a different way than witch magic.

Now and then the ghost dog would bark at her or lick her hand. Or the cat would meow and float upward to lick her cheek with its sandpapery tongue. It was as if they were trying to tell her something.

"Please, just go away!" she'd tell them. But they'd just answer with more barks and meows that she couldn't understand. *Sigh.*

"I don't understand ghost-speak," she informed them. "I wish I did, though. Because I have a feeling you'll only go away when I finally get whatever it is you're trying to tell me."

Both the cat and dog bobbed their heads as if to agree. She guessed that meant she was stuck with them. But for how long?

All during Charms class, the ghost cat slept curled around her neck like a collar, purring. The dog roamed around, sniffing everyone. A few students reacted to this. They would rub or scratch the place the dog had nosed as if they'd felt something. Others didn't seem to notice anything.

In third-period Curse Making and Breaking class, Hecate and her classmates practiced cursing assorted objects. *Hmm. Curses.* That made her wonder about something. Could these ghost animals be a sign that *she* was cursed? If so, their teacher Ms. Malediction might actually be able to rid her of the curse.

After class, Hecate approached her desk. "Ms. Mal?" she asked once the other students had headed off to lunch. "I was wondering if you'd have time to check me for symptoms of a curse? I've begun, um, sort of seeing ghosts today."

That got Ms. Malediction's attention. "Oh dear!" Right away, the teacher whipped out a magnifying glass. She examined Hecate through it from every possible angle. Then she dipped her fingertips into powders and potions to draw symbols such as stars and tic-tac-toe on Hecate's cheeks and hands. She checked her fingernails closely and peered into her eyes and ears.

While this was going on, Hecate chattered about what had happened in the cemetery. The teacher listened intently, but punctuated Hecate's story now and then with worried mutters, such as "Hmm," "Oh, dear," and "I've never seen that before."

"What's this?" Ms. Malediction asked at last. The teacher held up a mirror so Hecate could see her own reflection.

"Oh no! It's back!" Hecate exclaimed upon seeing her own face. The glitter had reappeared! Just like last night. Only this time it was on her nose. As she watched, it faded, then disappeared.

"You've had this before?" Ms. Mal inquired.

Hecate nodded. "On my arm. Last night. But it went away."

"This is worrisome," the teacher announced as she began putting her tools away. "Good thing you requested a checkup. Because I do see evidence of a possible curse. However, it's beyond my capabilities to break it."

Now, that *was* worrisome! Hecate chewed her lower lip. "So what should I do?"

"Since your grandmother, Ms. Hecate, is the Spell-ology teacher at Mount Olympus Academy, I suggest you visit her for help before this curse gets worse," Ms. Malediction replied.

Hecate blinked at her in surprise. "Huh? Who told you about her?"

"A student in my last class period mentioned that

you were related. Since Ms. Hecate is a goddess, she's far more powerful than I when it comes to defeating curses," explained Ms. Mal.

"But wouldn't I need an invitation to go to Mount Olympus?" asked Hecate. "Even though Ms. Hecate is my . . . er . . . grandmother?" She'd heard that Zeus, who was principal of MOA as well as King of the Gods and Ruler of the Heavens, didn't take kindly to random people just showing up.

"Normally, yes," her teacher replied. "But under the circumstances—that you may be cursed and need Ms. Hecate's expertise to find a cure—Zeus likely won't have a problem with you visiting without a formal invitation."

Hecate shuddered. Would she have to actually meet Zeus if she went there? She'd heard that he sometimes accidentally shocked students with little bolts of electricity that shot from his fingertips!

Ms. Malediction misinterpreted Hecate's shudder. "Don't worry. I'm sure your grandmother will know what to do, and you'll be fine in no time. Here, I'll write you a travel pass." She opened her desk drawer and pulled out a small textscroll.

Grandmother. Hecate gulped. She hated to let her teacher believe that, but if she admitted it wasn't true, she might not be allowed to seek help at MOA. And it sounded as if her condition required a powerful expert to treat it.

"Um, okay." Hecate shuffled from one booted foot to the other, her eyes avoiding Ms. Malediction's. The teacher pulled out a feather pen and a bottle of ink and began to write.

"I've heard Zeus has a fearsome temper," Hecate said, unable to let that worry go. "Are you sure he won't be mad if I show up unexpectedly? I mean, he's in charge of thunderbolts. Who knows what could happen?" And since she wasn't actually Ms. Hecate's granddaughter, it was probably extra foolish to appear at MOA without permission!

"The King of the Gods is a fair ruler," Ms. Mal reassured her. "He'll understand the importance of your visit once you explain. Oh, and please ask your grandmother if she might like to visit Hexwitch sometime and give a lecture. I would be so very glad to meet her."

Hecate's fingers rose to the pentagram patch on her school uniform. Unconsciously, she tapped the point that represented honesty. She felt awful that she wasn't living up to that ideal right now. Far from it. She knew she should admit to making up the relationship between her and Ms. Hecate. She might have done so, too, only she couldn't bear having her teachers find out she was a liar. They would be so disappointed in her!

Just then, the ghost cat knocked Ms. Malediction's crystal ball off her desk with a swish of its tail. As the ball rolled around on the floor, the ghost dog began chasing it and barking. When it rolled toward the teacher, she picked it up and placed it back on her desk, sending Hecate a worried look.

"The ghosts did that," Hecate informed her.

The teacher nodded, then handed her a pass to miss school and travel to Mount Olympus for as long as necessary. "Get going, dear. The sooner you're cured, the better."

Hecate didn't really want to go, but if she truly was cursed (as it seemed she must be), she needed the help that only Ms. Hecate could provide. If she didn't give this plan a try, she could be stuck with this dumb glitter and ghost-animal curse forever!

5 The Game

After grabbing a quick lunch, Hecate filled her bag with some extra blank papyrus squares and the piece of charcoal from last night. Then she strung a bunch of papyrus fact-card necklaces around her throat. Somehow, simply wearing these was a comfort! When she set off on her trip, the ghost cat and ghost dog followed, padding along at her heels.

A few minutes down the front path, she paused

and turned to glance back at her school. It was made of black stone and had many towers. The central one was by far the largest and had a pointy roof shaped like a witch's hat, which was dotted with their dorm rooms' many small windows. She felt so lucky to go here. It was hextastic!

Hecate glanced at a nearby sign on a large rack that was half filled with brooms. It read:

Broom Parking.

Violators Will Be Toad.

Too bad she hadn't earned her own riding-broom yet. She hoped she would, someday! Turning, she gazed at Mount Olympus rising majestically in the distance. Mount Olympus Academy was located at the tip-top of that mountain. Since she would have to walk all the way there, it was going to take half of forever to reach it.

If only she'd never met those ghosts last night. *Wait!* Was it possible the strange things that were happening had nothing to do with Hecate's birthday and turning twelve? Melinoe did have magical powers, after all. Had she put a glitter-and-ghost curse on her? If so, that girl's name should be changed to *Mean*linoe. But maybe that meant Hecate didn't have to go all the way to MOA. If this stuff was Melinoe's doing, maybe she could simply convince her to reverse the curse.

Thinking this worth a try, Hecate detoured to the pet cemetery. Fortunately, it didn't look so creepy during the daytime. It was actually rather pretty with its ivy, flowers, and gravestones. Unfortunately, its front gate was locked.

"Melinoe?" she called, peering through the gate's iron bars. No response. Though she called

and called, the girl never answered. "Well, this was a dead end," she said to the cat and dog. "Time to head for Mount Olympus."

As she set out again, she sighed. "I wish there were another, faster way that I could get to MOA, besides a broom. Any thoughts?" she asked the two animals trailing her. Although she didn't expect any replies, she did get an idea when the cat twitched its whiskers at her.

"Hey! That's it! I'll try a whisk-her spell." Hecate wrinkled her brows and gazed curiously at the cat. "Did you do that on purpose to give me the idea?"

The cat grinned, showing its alarmingly sharp teeth.

"Okay, rule number one for our trip. No smiling. Either of you," she told both ghost animals. Then she said a spell meant to whisk her to her destination.

"Whisk me far. And away.

Fly me off to MOA!"

Whoosh! Immediately, she was pulled from the path and . . . whisked back to her dorm room at Hexwitch! The ghost animals were whisked right along with her.

"Well, that didn't work," she grumbled. What had the spell thought she'd meant by MOA? My Own Area? My Own Abode? Maybe it would help if she made things clearer. She tried again, rushing her words out in her haste to be off:

"Whisk me to the Academy.

Zoom! Whoosh! Scurry!

To the top of Mount Olympus.

Please, spell, do hurry!"

Her second whisk-her spell landed her high in an olive tree alongside the road. Again, the ghost animals had come along. They even wound up in the tree with her! The cat was on the lowest branch and was able to jump down easily.

However, Hecate was seated on a high branch with the ghost dog in her lap. It bared its scary-looking teeth at her and growled. *Grr!*

"Hey, did you forget trip-rule number one? Get off me!" she ordered in a shaky voice. But then she realized it couldn't get down on its own. So she reined in her fear long enough to wrap an arm around it, climb down, and set it on the ground. When it licked her hand in gratitude, an odd, warm happiness filled her. These ghost animals might be scary, but it seemed that sometimes they could also be good company.

"Okay, magic spell," she muttered. "You got me to the *top* of something, all right. But it was a *tree*, not Mount Olympus. Let's try again." She repeated her second spell, taking care to say each word slowly and clearly.

Yes! That whisk-her spell worked! Sort of. It whisked her in the right direction, but only as far as the first crossroads—a place where the road she was on intersected another road.

"Still, it saved some time," she said to her two furry companions. Straightaway, several mortal travelers came to the crossroads from different directions. They stopped to chat.

"Talking to yourself?" asked one, who must've overheard her. She guessed he was a farmer since he was carrying a basket of vegetables, probably taking them to a food market.

“Where are you heading?” asked the other traveler before Hecate could answer. This lady was nicely dressed and carried a shoulder bag stuffed full of papers. She was obviously traveling on some business errand. The two strangers glanced at Hecate’s pointy black hat, but didn’t remark on it. She figured it was obvious to them that she was a witch, though. Some mortals were scared of witches; others (like these) weren’t.

However, like the witches back at school, neither mortal appeared aware of the ghost animals tagging along with her. Even though the dog was sniffing them and the cat was winding around their ankles!

Suddenly, there came a flash of light. The mortals didn’t seem to notice it—or the third ghost animal that appeared out of nowhere. A ghost ferret! Hecate knew from her fact collection that ferrets were a part of the weasel family. And they had a reputation for being mischievous. This one sure seemed to be. It had arrived sitting on the unsuspecting woman's head!

The farmer pointed to the sky, drawing everyone's attention. "Oh look, a rainbow!"

"How pretty!" said the woman. When she tilted her head to gaze at it, the surprised ferret had to scramble to keep its perch.

Hecate laughed and then tried to turn the laugh into a cough when the lady raised an eyebrow at her. The woman obviously didn't feel the weight of her new furry, er, *hat*.

Feeling embarrassed, Hecate blurted, "Did you know that the name of the goddess of the rainbow is . . ." But at the last moment she stopped herself from saying what it was. Because it occurred to her that this was the perfect chance to try out her new game and see if mortals enjoyed it.

"Do either of you know the name of the goddess of rainbows?" she asked the travelers. "I'll give you some hints. Is it Persephone? Iris? Or Pandora?" Instead of looking at her as if she were weird for asking such a question (which was what Jinx surely would have done), the mortals played along.

"Pandora?" guessed the farmer.

"Pandora's not a goddess. She's mortal," the woman told him, shaking her head. This time the ferret wrapped its forepaws tightly in her hair to keep from falling off. Unaware, the woman calmly added, "The answer is Iris."

"Correct," said Hecate.

The woman smiled, obviously pleased she'd been

right. Uninterested in facts, the dog left the road to investigate the nearby field. Meanwhile, the cat curled up next to the bag Hecate had set down by the crossroads signpost, and started grooming its fur.

"Give us another one," the farmer requested. "I want a chance to redeem myself. Just in case Zeus is listening in from the heavens. I don't want him to think badly of me, since I do know *some* things about the gods and goddesses."

"Okay," said Hecate, happy that they liked her game. "I've written a lot of my fact questions down," she said, tugging at her necklace. Just as she pulled off two papyrus squares, a family of four walked up to join them. The two young children were carrying scrollbooks, and she guessed they were on their way home from school. At this point, the ferret decided to burrow into the lady's bag to investigate its contents. Meanwhile, the cat wandered over to inspect everyone's boots or sandals.

The farmer and businesswoman enthusiastically explained that they were playing a game Hecate had created. At first the newcomers seemed only mildly interested in trying it.

Forging ahead, however, Hecate read one of her papyrus squares aloud. "'What's the name of Zeus's flying horse—Pegasus, Perseus, or Pigasus?'"

"Pegasus!" shouted all six travelers, including the children. Zeus's white winged horse was both well-known and popular! After that easy question, the new family became a bit more excited about the game.

But before Hecate could read another question from her necklace, the farmer held out his hand for the square and asked, "Okay if I do the next one?" Hecate nodded and gave it to him.

He scanned it quickly, then turned to the others. "It's not about immortals," he told them. "But see if you know the answer anyway: 'About how many hours do cats sleep each day? Eight, twelve, or sixteen?'"

With sudden interest, the ghost cat raised its paw. Hecate grinned. Of course it would know the answer!

The other five travelers made guesses. Only one guessed the correct answer—sixteen—but all seemed eager to keep playing. More travelers came along. They soon grew keen to play as well. It was nice to have her facts appreciated for a change! The travelers all took turns reading the questions and letting others guess the answers.

"I have to get going," Hecate told them after a while. Hearing this, the ferret poked its head up from the businesswoman's bag and then jumped down to the ground. The dog and cat wandered over to Hecate too.

"I'll leave some of my game questions for you and other travelers who come along, though," Hecate continued. "Maybe they'll enjoy them too."

She hung a fact necklace on one of the nails that was sticking out from the crossroads signpost. Apparently, travelers had posted messages, announcements, and ads here before, and the nails they'd used remained long after those were gone.

As she walked away carrying her bag, Hecate heard a traveler use one of her papyrus squares to quiz the others: "'Which Titan was Zeus's dad? Cronus? Oceanus? Or Hyperion?'"

The answer was Cronus! However, Hecate didn't wait to hear if anyone guessed right. She whisk-her-spelled herself away (which undoubtedly surprised the travelers!). Her spell took her and the three ghost animals only as far as the next crossroads.

"Guess I'll have to repeat my spell at every crossroads," she told the cat, dog, and ferret. "Still, it's faster than walking to the Academy."

No other travelers were in sight here. But more would pass this way eventually. So, since mortals at the last intersection had enjoyed her game, she hung another of her necklaces on a nail she found hammered into the signpost. She continued to do this at each crossroads she came to.

After five crossroads in all, Hecate and the ghost animals finally got whisked off . . . to a hallway! Inside a school? Could this be . . . Mount Olympus

Academy? "Well," she murmured to herself. "I didn't expect this. I thought I'd arrive outside the front door and have to knock."

Instead she now stood smack in the doorway of a classroom. When she heard the cat, dog, and ferret chasing each other behind her on the marble-tiled hallway, she turned to look. Outside a window at the far end of the hall she could see Helios, the sun god, in the distance. He was dipping his horse-drawn carriage to sail the sun lower toward the horizon. Once it set, night would fall.

Hecate looked up. Bright, colorful paintings on the hall's domed ceiling detailed the glorious exploits of the goddesses and gods. Wow! It was the most magnificent painting she'd ever seen. The hall was empty of students and teachers. If this *was* Mount

Olympus Academy, classes must be over for the day. However, she could hear voices coming from within the classroom.

In a way she was at another crossroads, she realized. The long hall and the entrance into the classroom formed a sort of intersection, with three possible directions she could go. Up or down the hall, or into the classroom. She turned to read a sign on the wall next to the classroom's open door. It read: SPELL-OLOGY. That was the class Ms. Hecate taught! Despite the mistakes and delays along the way, the whisk-her spell had somehow known where she wanted to end up. Perfect!

Maybe it would only take a few minutes for Ms. Hecate to cure her curse! Eagerly, Hecate took a step forward and leaned to poke her head inside the room. The whiteboard at its front was covered with written incantations. A small crystal ball and magic wand rested atop each student desk.

A half dozen students about her same age were gathered to one side of the largest desk, which had to be the teacher's. They were talking among themselves while decorating a big bulletin board on the wall beyond the large desk. Some kind of special project, she guessed. Either that or they were just helping out the teacher.

A flash of light came before Hecate could speak up. Two more ghost animals—a peacock with beautiful feathers and a pink pig—appeared out of nowhere to stand on either side of her! She let out a surprised squeak and leaped forward into the room. Just as quickly, she tried to back out before she could be noticed. Too late!

Her squeak had drawn attention. She froze in her tracks when a grown-up voice boomed out, "Who are you, witch-girl? And what are you doing here at Mount Olympus Academy?"

Oh, scraggletwix! That voice did not sound like it could belong to Ms. Hecate. Not at all.

6
Mount Olympus

THE FIVE GHOST ANIMALS (CAT, DOG, FERRET, peacock, and pig) rushed ahead of Hecate as she hesitantly entered the Spell-ology classroom. Immediately they began to frolic and investigate everything they saw. She wished she could feel as carefree as they seemed to!

In the meantime, the six students turned away from the bulletin board. They gazed at her in surprise, their eyes going to the black hat that marked her as a witch. Too nervous to meet their eyes, she studied their bulletin board instead. There was a big poster tacked on it with large decorative letters that read:

WELCOME BACK!

We Missed You, Ms. Hecate!

Huh? Did this mean the Spell-ology teacher wasn't here after all? Hecate wondered in dismay. After she'd come all this way?

All at once, her breath caught, because she noticed the god who must've spoken to her a moment ago. He was over behind the teacher's desk, standing nearly seven feet tall, with bulging muscles everywhere. Wide, flat, gold bracelets encircled his thick wrists. His piercing blue gaze narrowed as he glared . . . at her!

This had to be the King of the Gods—and MOA principal—Zeus himself! Hecate shivered.

"Well? ANSWER ME!" Zeus thundered. He pointed a long finger in her direction. "Who are you, and what are you doing here without my invitation?"

"I'm Hecate from Hexwitch School," she replied in a gush of words. Then she began to rattle off facts about him as if they were a shield that might protect her from his wrath. "You're Zeus. You grew up on the island of Crete. You were raised in a cave in the care of a goat named Amalthea and some nymphs." She put a hand over her mouth to stop herself from spouting more random information.

Luckily, Zeus seemed pleased that she knew so much about him. For about two seconds. Then he was back to frowning, with both arms crossed over his huge chest. The students in the room studied

her with interest. Were they fascinated by the coincidence of her having the same name as their teacher?

Suddenly, a dog howled, pulling everyone's attention. *Ar-ooo!*

"Quiet!" roared Zeus.

"You can hear that? The dog howling, I mean?" Hecate asked him. She glanced around for the ghost dog and spotted it chasing the ghost peacock and ghost pig. The cat and ferret were calmly sitting on the teacher's desk, having a stare-off.

"Unfortunately, yes," said Zeus. He winced at the sound of more howls. Then three very real *live* dogs came scampering into the room. These were the ones that had been doing the howling, not the ghost dog!

"Quiet!" Zeus shouted again. Ignoring his command, all three dogs—a bloodhound, a beagle, and a greyhound—lifted their heads and howled in unison. *Ar-ooo!* Restlessly, they roamed the room, snuffling excitedly.

They must sense the presence of the ghost animals, thought Hecate. And it seemed she was right, because soon they gave chase, tracking those five ghostly creatures either by scent or sight, or maybe a little of both. The ghost animals thought this a fun game. They floated and flitted above and between the hounds, teasing them by letting them get close, then jumping out of reach. This caused the hounds to bump into each other and knock things over. *Crash!* A pile of textscrolls on a student desk fell to the floor.

A dark-haired girl came running over to the hounds, calling, "Suez! Amby! Nectar! Behave!"

Hecate held up a finger. "Um, I'll be back in a

sec," she said, although no one was really paying her any attention now. Quietly, she slipped out into the hall. As she'd expected, all five ghost animals followed. Once they were in the hall too, she shouted, "Stay!" Then she jumped back into the classroom, shutting the door behind her.

But in two seconds they were back in the room again. Those disobedient ghost animals had simply passed through the walls like magic!

Frustrated, Hecate momentarily forgot her fear of animals. She pointed to the door. "Go," she ordered sternly. "Stay out in the hall till I come for you." Looking droopy, they nevertheless obeyed her and disappeared back through the walls. She could hear them snuffling and howling out in the hall. But no one else seemed to.

Maybe because the three real dogs inside the

room were making too much noise! They'd begun sniffing the door, whining. Obviously, they sensed that their new playmates were just beyond it.

By this time, everyone in the room was staring at Hecate. Because she'd been speaking to invisible animals, no doubt. "Um, oh, sorry. Just talking to myself," she explained with a weak grin. She spread her hands in apology. "Crazy, huh?"

The dark-haired girl went over and patted her hounds to quiet them. "Wish I knew what's got you guys so overexcited," she said.

The girl's black hair was gathered in a gold band high on her head, and a quiver full of arrows and an archery bow were slung over her shoulder. Hecate knew this had to be Artemis, goddessgirl of the hunt, forest, and moon. Artemis's three best friends were here too.

Although none of them would know Hecate, she recognized them. There was Persephone, the goddessgirl of flowers and plants, with long curly red hair and green eyes. And Aphrodite, the goddessgirl of love and beauty. She was extraordinarily beautiful and had golden hair and bright blue eyes. Athena was the brainy one, with blue-gray eyes and brown hair. And she was Zeus's daughter, too! Identical gold necklaces with dangling double-*G*-shaped charms hung from the necks of all four girls.

Being around these goddessgirls, Hecate couldn't help feeling a little awestruck. They were like pop stars! The four most popular goddessgirls at MOA. Everyone on Earth and Mount Olympus knew of them. Like Hecate, Greek mortals and immortals read a publication called *Teen Scrollazine*, which was delivered to them every week. It was full of news, information, and also gossip about the exploits of immortals.

Hecate wasn't sure who the other two girls in the room were. She hadn't had a chance to look at them closely before they'd turned to work on the bulletin board again.

Tap, tap, tap. Uh-oh! Zeus's arms were still crossed, and he was tapping one of his large, gold-sandaled feet. He scowled at Hecate. "Well? SPEAK! And your reason for coming here had better be good."

Hecate jerked in fear. Her eyes darted around the room for a place to hide. Would he strike her with a thunderbolt if he didn't like her answer? She'd better make it *especially* good—fast!

"I'm Ms. Hecate's granddaughter," she lied speedily. Because she was more than a little afraid of Zeus, to be honest. (And, really, who wouldn't be?) Plus, she was worried he might not let her stay. Which she needed to do. At least long enough for Ms. Hecate to come back from wherever she'd gone and reverse this curse!

Zeus cocked his head at her, his blue gaze suspicious. "What? I don't think so. Ms. Hecate doesn't have any children. So how could she have a granddaughter?"

"Um, well, you'll have to ask her about that," Hecate replied lamely.

Just then, a ray of Helios's dwindling sunlight shot in through a window. It glinted off the jagged gold thunderbolt on Zeus's belt buckle, making it gleam. It was a reminder of the power he possessed. He could zap her into oblivion right where she stood, if he chose to!

Flustered, Hecate began to spout random facts

about thunder and lightning. "Did you know that the study of thunder is called brontology and the study of lightning is called fulminology? And the fear of lightning is called keraunophobia or astraphobia?" she asked him.

Zeus stared at her with an openmouthed look of astonishment. Was it because it amazed him that she knew such information? Or was he simply surprised (and maybe a little weirded out) that she was telling him all this? Probably the latter. But that didn't stop her mouth from jabbering more facts without her permission. "When a lightning bolt flashes, it creates a sound wave called thunder. Lightning can heat nearby air until it's five times hotter than the sun. Oh, and lightning never strikes twice in the same place," she babbled on breathlessly.

Zeus planted his meaty fists at his hips and stared

at her even harder. Did he think her annoying? Would he strike her with a thunderbolt just to shut her up?

"Quit talking," she mumbled to herself. She gritted her teeth to keep more facts from escaping.

Then she smiled wide at him, vaguely aware that the girls in the room were staring at her with similar looks of astonishment. "Sorry. You're a big deal," she told Zeus. "So I'm kind of nervous."

"You're quite knowledgeable about thunder and lightning," Zeus told her with surprising calm. "However, that last one is just a myth. I *can* make lightning strike in the same location as many times as I like."

"What's the difference between lightning and thunder?" one of the two girls Hecate hadn't identified earlier asked now. Her bangs were shaped like question marks.

Question marks? Hecate almost snapped her fingers as she realized that this girl had to be Pandora! A mortal, she was the only one of the six girls in the room whose skin didn't subtly shimmer. Her curiosity was infamous, though! It had once led her to open a box of trouble bubbles here at MOA, with near-disastrous results.

"Lightning is a high-voltage electric discharge. Thunder is the loud clap caused by the rapid expansion of the air surrounding the path of a lightning bolt," Zeus explained to her easily.

Hecate's mind raced, her eyes flicking between him and Pandora. Since Pandora had been allowed to stay at MOA, even after the trouble she'd caused, surely Zeus would let Hecate remain till Ms. Hecate returned. Right?

Nope. She was wrong. "No one is allowed into

Mount Olympus Academy without my invitation," Zeus told her firmly. "Return home. When Ms. Hecate gets back, I'll check out your story."

"Please, won't you let me wait for her here? I've come a really long way." Hecate glanced at the four popular goddessgirls, sending them her best pleading look.

"If she tells me it's true that she's your grandmother, I'll invite you back," Zeus assured her.

Well, that wasn't going to happen. Because her story wasn't true! Shoulders slumped in disappointment, Hecate trudged for the door.

But then Athena's voice caused her to turn back with renewed hope. "It's almost dark out, Dad. What's the harm in letting her stay? At least for dinner. And maybe a sleepover in the girls' dorm tonight?"

"Ms. Hecate probably *would* be disappointed," Artemis agreed.

"Finding out her granddaughter wasn't welcomed here won't be much of a nice welcome back for our teacher," added Persephone.

"Persephone's spending the night with her mom. So Hecate could stay in our room," added Aphrodite.

Hecate hadn't dared hope that her pleading look would be so effective. She didn't even know these goddessgirls. Did they really believe her story about being Ms. Hecate's granddaughter? Maybe they were just giving her the benefit of the doubt. Still, they had no reason to take her side. She had a feeling that they were just supernice. Which was, well, supernice!

"It's true that Hecate *has* traveled a long way to

get here. All the way from Earth," said the sixth girl in the room.

"How did you know that?" Hecate asked, blinking at her in surprise. The girl stepped forward. She had orange-glossed lips and short, spiked hair of the same color. "You're Pheme! The goddessgirl of gossip, right?"

The girl grinned and confirmed her guess. "Yep, that's me. I pride myself on scooping all the news that happens on Earth and Mount Olympus." As she spoke, her words puffed out in cloud letters that slowly rose around her to fade away overhead. This was one way she helped spread news!

"Mortals and immortals tell me stuff," Pheme went on. "They can't help it. Like today, a mortal mentioned that he'd met a young witch, who then magically disappeared, at a crossroads on Earth. Was it you?"

"Probably," said Hecate. "I did meet travelers. And I used a whisk-her spell to get me here faster." Pheme, she knew, snooped in everyone's business. And she used what she learned to write a popular gossip column in *Teen Scrollazine*. Knowing this, Hecate gulped when Pheme stepped closer and began to examine her in detail. Maybe she was planning to describe her to others at some point . . . in her column. *Ye gods!* Hecate wasn't sure she liked that idea!

"So, what do you say, Dad?" Athena cocked her head at Zeus and sent him a soft smile.

He sighed. "Oh, all right. You know I have a hard time denying you anything, daughter. Hecate can stay one night with you girls in your dorm. But if she makes *any* trouble, she's gone."

"I won't. Promise." Hecate did a little happy dance. Then she asked, "So where *is* Ms. Hec—I mean my grandmother, anyway?"

Zeus shrugged his big shoulders, causing the tunic he wore to almost rip under the strain of his muscles. "She didn't say. Off on some kind of mission. She wasn't sure when she'd be back." He turned away, found an ink pen, and began signing his name (big) to the WELCOME BACK poster on the bulletin board. There were lots of names on it already. Her fake grandmother was obviously well liked!

Seeing Hecate's interest, Aphrodite waved a hand to indicate the poster. "We made this to surprise Ms. Hecate when she returns."

Persephone's green eyes lit up. "Yeah, it's not just any old welcome-back sign. We added magic touches. Watch this." She went over and pushed her

fingertip against the letter *W* in the word "welcome." Wildflowers sprang out of the top of the letter.

"That's so awesome!" Hecate declared, clapping her hands in delight.

"And a heart will appear if you push on the *H* in Ms. Hecate's name," Aphrodite told her. "*H* as in 'heart.' I came up with that one."

"I *looove* it!" Hecate joked, smiling to let her know she really did.

After finishing his enormous signature, Zeus turned to Hecate. His blue eyes flashed with excitement as he pointed to one of the two jagged thunderbolt-shaped *E*s in the word "welcome." "And guess what appears when you push either *E*?" he asked her. He sounded as eager as a little boy!

"Um . . . something really fun?" Hecate asked uncertainly.

"Try it and see," he commanded.

Her and her big mouth. No way did she want to touch either thunderbolt-shaped *E*. A big bolt of lightning would probably blast out of the letter to strike her! But what choice did she have?

Doing as Zeus ordered, Hecate went over to the poster. She squeezed her eyes closed and leaned her face away from it. Then she reached out and pushed the first *E* with a fingertip.

Zzzt! She jumped away as dozens of white zigzag sparks blasted out of the letter! For a few seconds, the thunderbolt *E* turned into a sparkling fountain of light! She breathed a sigh of relief. No dangerous shocks. It was just a light show. A really cool one!

She spread her arms wide. "That's de-*light*-ful!" she proclaimed with enthusiasm. Because it really was!

Zeus smiled big. "It was my idea," he boasted with a huge grin. Abruptly, he turned on his heel and strode for the door. "Well, I'm off. Work to do! King of the Gods, Ruler of the Heavens, principal of MOA, and all that, you know."

After he left, Pandora turned to the group of students. "Who's hungry?"

Everyone raised their hands.

7 Goddessgirls

MOUNT OLYMPUS ACADEMY'S CAFETERIA WAS filled with immortal students—all of them beautiful, powerful, and awesome, with softly shimmering skin. There were a few mortal students too, recognizable since their skin *didn't* shimmer.

The minute the six MOA girls and Hecate walked inside, Pheme spotted some trouble brewing. "Ooh! Poseidon and Ares are arguing," she said, looking intrigued. "Sounds like it's over which weapon is fiercer in battle, a trident or a spear. See you guys later!" With that, Pheme took off for the boys' table in search of gossip.

Wow, that girl must have super hearing, thought Hecate, who hadn't been able to hear anything the boys were saying. Made sense, though. That ability befitted a goddessgirl who was always searching out the latest news.

Hecate and the other girls headed for the dinner line. The five ghost animals trailed them, and Artemis's dogs in turn followed them, sniffing and snuffling.

Up ahead, an eight-armed cafeteria lady was serving students from clay bowls decorated with black-silhouetted figures. "Hi, Ms. Okto," the goddessgirls greeted her when it was their turn to grab trays and join the line.

The busy lady threw them a quick smile. "What'll it be, girls?"

"We brought a visitor," Athena told her, gesturing toward Hecate. "Could you explain to her what everything is?"

"Be glad to," Ms. Okto replied. As the MOA girls moved through the dinner line ahead of Hecate, Ms. Okto rattled off the names of the many foods on offer, using a big spoon in one of her eight hands to point them out. At the same time, she dished up food for other students with her remaining seven hands.

Hecate's eyes went wide at the many food and drink choices on display. "We mostly eat stuff like Eye of Newt or Toad-in-a-Box at my school," she told the other girls.

"What? That sounds, um, interesting," said Persephone, her head jerking back in surprise.

"Don't worry, it's tasty. And there aren't really newts or toads in it," Hecate explained. Moving through the line, she chose a bowl of celestial soup with noodles shaped like planets and stars. Then she added, "The Hexwitch cafeteria staff are witches, and so they can make our food taste like anything we want."

"Even like ambrosia or nectar?" asked Pandora.

"Maybe. If they knew what those tasted like," Hecate told her. "I've never had them, though, and I'm guessing they haven't either."

"Well, you *must* try them while you're here!" Athena practically commanded. "Zeus doesn't allow anyone to take them outside Mount Olympus, so this is your big chance."

As Hecate already knew, all immortals ate ambrosia and drank nectar, and these divine confections

kept them youthful. And, apparently, they came in many delicious forms. Acting on Athena's suggestion, she added an ambrosia salad and a carton of nectar to her tray.

When the girls settled at a round table with room for six, she tried both, first thing. "Mmm, delicious," she said, glancing up from her plate. Her eyes widened with shock and dismay when she noticed that the five ghost animals—the cat, dog, ferret, peacock, and pig—had been joined by two more: a wild-eyed monkey and a sharp-beaked raven! That made seven!

The monkey let out a high-pitched screech. Then it leaped to the ceiling in a single bound to swing from one of the chandeliers. *Caw!* went the raven. It zoomed upward to circle around the room. Hecate choked and began coughing right in the middle of her third sip of nectar. "What is happening here?"

she wailed, forgetting that everyone could hear her, but not see or hear these ghost animals.

Persephone gasped, her eyes going wide as she stared at Hecate. "You're suddenly glittery—that's what's happening!"

"Yeah, all over," added Artemis. She pointed her fork at Hecate and moved it in a circular motion.

"Huh?" Hecate looked down at herself. Both her arms now looked as if they'd been powdered with golden glitter. She tried rubbing the glitter off with her napkin. But it seemed permanent this time.

"Is it a rash or something?" Pandora asked.

Aphrodite shook her head, sending her long golden hair swaying. "I don't think so. I think it looks like you're a goddessgirl, Hecate!"

"What? No way," Hecate began.

But her attention was interrupted just then by a

growing cacophony of meows, barks, oinks, caws, and other animal sounds. The seven ghost animals and Artemis's dogs were running wild in the cafeteria! All the noise was making it hard to focus on what her new friends were saying. Still, no one else appeared to notice the ghosts. She did her best to tune them out.

"So I'm immortal now? Just like that?" She snapped her fingers and looked back at her new friends in question. "Seems hard to believe."

"You must be, though," Persephone told Hecate.

Athena nodded. "I found out I was a goddessgirl kind of suddenly too. I grew up on Earth thinking I was a mortal. Then one day Zeus sent me a letter-scroll telling me I was his daughter and commanding me to move to MOA to attend school. There had been weird hints that I was immortal before that,

but I didn't understand what they were trying to tell me. Once I drank nectar, though, my skin began to shimmer, and then I *knew*."

"Hmm," said Hecate. "There's been some weirdness in my life lately too." Like ghost animals following her around! She gazed at her arms, rolling them back and forth to study how the glitter shimmered under the light. If this was caused by her being a goddessgirl, that must mean it had nothing to do with a curse at all!

Still, what was up with these ghost animals following her? If more kept appearing, she was going to wind up with a *zoo*. It made no sense! She was *not* an animal person. So even if she *was* a goddessgirl, she still needed to break this ghost-animal curse or whatever it was. Would Ms. Hecate have the skills to cure her and make them disappear? She really hoped so!

"How can I be positive I'm a goddessgirl, though? Wait. I know!" she said before anyone could offer an answer.

She turned to face Artemis, who was seated diagonally across the table. "Shoot me with one of your arrows," she told the girl.

"What? No!" Artemis hugged her quiver of arrows as if fearing Hecate might try to grab one and do the deed herself.

"Why not? If I'm truly immortal, an arrow won't hurt me, right?" Hecate reasoned.

"An arrow won't *kill* you," Persephone said carefully.

"But that doesn't mean it won't *hurt*—a lot—if Artemis shoots you," Athena explained.

"Oh," said Hecate, her shoulders drooping. "I see. So becoming immortal can't completely protect

someone from harm." How disappointing! Even if it turned out to be true that she was a goddessgirl, it seemed that she would still have to fear the world around her. (Not that fear wasn't a good thing at times. It could keep one from doing things that could be harmful. It just wasn't fun being *overly* fearful.)

Woof! Woof! Woof! The barks of Artemis's three dogs sounded excited and playful. Wagging their tails, they'd stopping chasing the ghost animals and had begun to frisk around the cafeteria with them instead. It appeared that they were all becoming pals.

"Guys, calm down!" Artemis called to her hounds. Digging in her quiver, she located some dog treats. The sound of them hitting the floor got their attention. All three loped over and scrambled around under the girls' table to gobble them. As the hounds proceeded to scarf the treats down in record time,

Aphrodite pulled the hem of her chiton out of their way, looking a bit displeased. Not a dog fan, it seemed.

"What's up with your hounds tonight?" Pandora wondered aloud to Artemis. Hecate was beginning to notice that most things this curious girl said were in the form of questions.

"No clue," Artemis replied. She scrunched her face in puzzlement as, having finished the treats, her pets tore off to race around the cafeteria again.

If Artemis only knew her hounds were playing with a pack of ghost animals! Hecate briefly considered telling her newfound friends what was going on. However, Zeus had said he didn't want any trouble from her. He would definitely consider ghost animals to be trouble. What if these girls felt obligated to tell him? He might send her home. She couldn't take that chance.

"Guess I'd better take my dogs outside," said

Artemis, pushing away her empty plate. "Ms. Okto doesn't look very happy about them running around."

Sure enough, the eight-armed cafeteria lady was glaring at the frisky dogs as she continued to dish up food for students. Artemis stood and whistled for her dogs. "C'mon, boys!" Reluctantly, they obeyed and followed her outside. Luckily, the ghost animals went with them! Maybe playing in the fresh air would wear them out. Or maybe they'd never return. Hecate could only hope!

Aphrodite stood too, and looked at Persephone, Athena, Pandora, and Hecate. "If you guys are all done eating, we should get going."

"Where to now?" Hecate asked, after they'd all carried their trays to the tray return.

Athena pointed a finger upward. "Girls' dorm is on the fourth floor. C'mon up!"

Minutes later, Hecate was hanging out with the four girls in the dorm room that Athena and Pandora shared. While Athena sat cross-legged on the floor, Aphrodite and Persephone each sat on one of the beds. Hecate was seated on one of the desk chairs and Pandora sat on the other. They'd left their door wide open, as had most other girls on the hall, and there was a constant stream of visitors stopping in to chat.

"Your room is *so* cute!" Hecate told Athena and Pandora when she got the chance.

"Thanks," said Athena. "All the rooms along our hall are identical, with two beds opposite each other, plus two closets and two built-in desks. But we can decorate them any way we want."

Pandora cocked her head at Hecate and asked, "Can you guess which half of our room belongs to which of us?"

Hecate glanced around, then pointed to one of the beds. "I'm guessing that side is yours, because of the question-mark design on the bedspread. And I'm guessing the other side is Athena's, because of the pictures of scientists, inventors, and philosophers tacked on the bulletin board on the wall there." Then she couldn't help mentioning a fact related to one of the brainy Greeks pictured. "Pythagoras's math theorem says that in a right triangle, the square of the hypotenuse—the longest side—is equal to the sum of the squares of the two shorter sides."

"You're *right*—just like the triangle in his theorem!" said Athena. Which cracked everyone up.

"So you guys room together?" Hecate asked

Aphrodite and Persephone once the giggles died down.

A goofy grin came over Persephone's face, and she sent a good-humored glance toward Aphrodite. "Actually, Aphrodite shares *her* room with her clothes. And with me when I sleep over, which is only half the time. Other nights I spend at my mom's house on Earth. She's Demeter, owner of the Daisies, Daffodils, and Floral Delights shop in the Immortal Marketplace."

Aphrodite grinned back, raising both hands palms-up. "What can I say? The goddessgirl of love and beauty *loves* clothes."

Hecate grinned at her and then said, "I wonder what I'll turn out to be the goddessgirl of?"

"Goddessgirl of witches?" suggested Pandora.

Hecate nodded thoughtfully. "Maybe, but—"

"In time, you'll discover what your goddessgirl gifts are," Persephone assured her.

"Yeah, like I did," said Athena.

Hecate found herself admiring these girls a lot. Athena for her brains and friendliness. Artemis for her bravery and confidence. Pandora for her questioning mind. And Aphrodite was beautiful, generous, and fun. However, Hecate felt especially drawn to Persephone. Although she was flowery and upbeat, her crush was widely known to be Hades, godboy of the Underworld. So she must have a dark side—something a witch like Hecate could relate to! Too bad she wouldn't have more than one night to get acquainted with everyone.

Just then, Persephone stood and announced, "Speaking of my mom, she's expecting me home every night this week. Gotta go, but I'll see you guys back

here in the morning for breakfast." Quickly, it was confirmed Hecate was borrowing her bed for the night.

After Persephone took off, Athena hopped up to sit on the bed she'd vacated and looked over at Hecate. "We already know an enchantress named Medea and a fortune-teller named Cassandra. But we've never met a witch. Sooo we were wondering . . ."

"Do you learn spells in school?" Pandora blurted.

"Sure," said Hecate. "Today in Incantations class I gave a mean mortal girl a mustache." This sent everyone into a fit of giggles. "A rash, too. We practice on mortals, but remove all our spells almost immediately."

Explaining that suddenly got Hecate thinking. Were whatever goddessgirl powers she now possessed strong enough to make the ghost animals permanently disappear? She'd hesitate to try. Because

if Ms. Malediction's spells weren't powerful enough, then any spells Hecate cast might only make things worse. Like what if she accidentally multiplied the number of ghost animals by a thousand or something? That was a horrifying thought!

Noticing some blue-and-gold pom-poms, Hecate picked one up and shook it, causing a rattling sound. "Are you guys on a cheer squad?" she asked.

Athena and Aphrodite nodded. "With Artemis, Persephone, and some others," Athena explained.

"I do flag team—do you have one of those at Hexwitch? Or a cheer squad?" asked Pandora.

Hecate shook her head, causing a lock of her wild black hair to fall across her face. "Nuh-uh, but there's a broom team that does flying acrobatics. I'm not on it," she told them. She was too embarrassed to admit that after a dozen tries she still hadn't mastered fly-

ing. Maybe that was something her new goddessgirl powers might eventually help her with, but she'd have to learn what they were and how to use them first. Which could take a while.

As she pushed the lock of hair back over her shoulder, her hands brushed her fact necklaces, making the squares rustle. Athena leaned forward. "What's up with your necklaces? We've been wondering about that, too."

"Oh, I have lots of these. I make them." Quickly Hecate explained how her fact game worked. "I left a necklace of game cards at each crossroads I came to on my way here today. To help travelers pass the time."

"I love that!" Aphrodite said, clapping in delight. "What a great icebreaker to help them get to know each other. A way for shy people to begin talking.

A game like that could start some romances." She sighed happily at the thought.

"I'm glad mortals seem to appreciate facts. Because I enjoy collecting them, but . . ." Hecate looked down, then shot the three girls a self-conscious glance.

"What?" asked Pandora.

Hecate shrugged. "Well, two witches at my school give me a hard time about my little hobby," she admitted. "One time, this girl Jinx made rude armpit noises and called them, er, 'fact farts.'"

"How mean!" Athena exclaimed. The other girls huffed in agreement.

As if to make Hecate feel better, Aphrodite admitted, "I once armpit-played a few fart songs myself. The sounds I made would normally have embarrassed me or any goddessgirl." This, of course, lightened the mood, and they all laughed. "Turned out

I was under the spell of a 'Rude' trouble bubble," she explained through her giggles. "One of the ones that escaped from a box Pandora opened."

"Yeah, I heard about that trouble-bubble box," said Hecate.

Athena sent her a tiny smile. "Everyone did. Because *Teen Scrollazine* published an article about it. We all did some *really* embarrassing things because of those bubbles! Even me. Don't ask."

Pandora reached over and nudged her shoulder in friendly apology. "Yeah, sorry about that, you guys. You understand I couldn't help myself, right? I *had* to open that box. I was practically *dying* of curiosity, you know?"

"Sure, and everything turned out okay," Athena assured her with a friendly smile.

"Mm-hm," Aphrodite added. "Especially since

one of those bubbles was filled with hope. And hope is always a good thing."

Probably eager to leave the subject of her bubble boo-boo, Pandora looked Hecate's way. "Will you tell us about your game?" she suggested.

"Really?" said Hecate. When the girls all nodded, she handed them one of her necklaces and let them read the papyrus squares as she explained how the game worked.

The girls were instantly drawn in and wanted to play. Especially the brainy Athena, who was hard to stump.

After they'd played a while, Athena offered Hecate some papyrus. That way, when the girls came up with new Q&A ideas now and then, she could add new squares to her necklaces. Hecate studied the piece of charcoal Melinoe had magically repaired

in the pet cemetery. Strangely, yet luckily, it never seemed to get smaller or break. Her spell must've changed it to last forever!

After playing the game for two hours, everyone began yawning. Soon Hecate trailed Aphrodite to her room to spend the night. She quickly discovered that this goddessgirl's room was also cutely decorated and very neat. Sparkly pink and red heart-shaped pillows were artfully arranged on each bed, and painted pink and red hearts decorated the walls.

"After all, I *am* the goddess of love!" Aphrodite reminded her with a laugh, having noticed Hecate eyeing everything.

"And of beauty," said Hecate, gesturing toward the items covering one of the two desks.

Aphrodite was naturally beautiful, but apparently

she loved trying out beauty products anyway. Her desk was half covered with rows of nail polish, lip gloss in every color, and dozens of eye shadows, blushes, and creams. When Hecate ventured closer to look, a magical silver-handled hairbrush jumped up from the desk. Hovering a few inches above a dish of ribbons and hair ornaments, it eyed her hopefully.

"I could give you a quick makeover if you want," Aphrodite suggested.

"Um, no thanks. No makeover for me," Hecate told her, backing away from the brush. "Especially if it involves a new hairstyle. Witches are supposed to have wild hair!" Looking a little disappointed, the hairbrush dropped back on the desk.

At her comment, Aphrodite looked downright flabbergasted. Flipping a lock of her own long, shiny golden hair over one shoulder, she went over to a closet. "Well, I can lend you a nightgown, at least." When she flung open its door, the clothes magically fluttered and swayed as if begging her to choose them.

"Wow! You *do* have a lot of clothes," said Hecate. But that really shouldn't have been a surprise. It was a well-known fact that Aphrodite set most fashion trends at Mount Olympus Academy. And those trends filtered down to Earth, too.

Aphrodite stroked a few of her chitons fondly. "Like Persephone hinted, I consider these outfits my almost roommates," she said, grinning at Hecate over one shoulder. "Artemis and I were roommates for a while, but dog hair and drool are not my thing. So she took the room next door."

Aphrodite went to her closet. "Choose one of my nightgowns for tonight," Aphrodite offered. "If you

don't like any of these, I have another closet with more over in Artemis's room."

"Thanks." Hecate set her bag and hat atop a shelf and quickly chose a black gown.

"How did I guess you'd pick that one!" said Aphrodite with a sweet laugh. Hecate couldn't help laughing too. "I don't wear black much myself—I prefer shades of pink—but it's good to have a full range of color choices in one's wardrobe."

Moments later, Hecate flopped onto Aphrodite's spare bed and slipped beneath its plush red velvet comforter. She ran a fingertip over one of the little white hearts stitched on it. And then she fell asleep.

Sometime in the night, she felt a warm weight on her feet. Peeking through the dimness, she saw that the ghost animals were back! The cat and ferret were sleeping on top of the comforter at the bottom of her

bed. The dog was curled up on the rug in the middle of the floor. The raven's beady eyes gleamed from where it perched on a high shelf on Aphrodite's side of the room. Although she didn't spot the peacock, pig, or monkey, she felt sure they were snuggled somewhere nearby. It seemed she was sort of getting used to them, because her eyes slowly closed again and she soon fell back asleep.

8 Fun Facts

HECATE WAS AWAKENED SATURDAY MORNING by a knock on Aphrodite's door. Persephone ducked her head inside the room, wearing a fresh chiton and some daisies in her hair. "Just got back from my mom's," she informed Hecate and Aphrodite, who were still in bed. "Should we get breakfast and maybe play the fact game later? I ran into Pandora just now, and she said the game was fun last night!"

"Sounds good," Aphrodite told her, standing to yawn and stretch her arms high.

Hecate was about to agree as well, but then her jaw dropped and her eyes bugged out. Because . . . was that a ghost unicorn standing next to Persephone? It looked just like the one from the pet cemetery! She sat up and blinked at it a few times. It didn't disappear.

"Oh no," she breathed. It was cute, but it was the size of a small pony, and its golden horn looked sharp, like it could skewer her and her new friends into a girl-kebab if it wanted! The unicorn glowed pink, Aphrodite's favorite color. Too bad Hecate couldn't off-load it on her. She'd probably love it! Unfortunately, these ghost animals seemed drawn to Hecate, though.

"If you don't like my plan, that's okay," Persephone told her, mistaking her words.

"Huh?" said Hecate, still distracted.

When the unicorn trotted out to investigate the hall, the rest of the ghost animals joined it to romp. Hecate could hear the three hounds barking excitedly from Artemis's room next door. No doubt they sensed the ghost animals' antics.

Just then, Artemis and Athena popped into Aphrodite's room too. To Hecate's surprise, they were *all* keen to play more of her game. It was a hit! There was only one problem.

"Sorry, but I don't have any more necklaces with me," Hecate told them as she rose from the bed too. "Just the ones with the fact cards we did last night. And you know all the answers to those."

"Can't we play with them anyway?" Artemis suggested. "Persephone and I won't know the answers, since we haven't gotten a chance to play yet."

Persephone turned pleading eyes on Hecate. "And you'll make more cards before you have to leave, right?"

"Don't worry. Zeus won't send her home anytime soon," Athena assured her. "She's still shimmering."

"Yeah! Which means she really is a goddessgirl now! One of us!" Aphrodite added happily.

"I am?" Did that mean she might eventually be invited to stay at MOA on a permanent basis? That would be like a dream come true! Yet she'd miss her teachers and friends at Hexwitch. *Hmm.*

After Hecate and Aphrodite got dressed and they all had breakfast, Aphrodite, Persephone, Pandora, and Artemis decided to play a quick card game in the dorm. Meanwhile, Athena took Hecate to speak to Zeus. It was time to find out where things stood, now that they knew Hecate was a goddessgirl.

As the two girls walked inside Zeus's outer office, Athena greeted the lady behind the desk. "Hi, Ms. Hydra." Ms. Hydra smiled at her. At least, one of her heads did: a sunny yellow one. She had nine heads in all, each a different color!

While the heads and Athena chatted briefly, Hecate turned her back on them to murmur to the eight ghost animals that had followed her here and were now exploring the office. "Be good. Zeus isn't someone we want to anger. Don't chew his sandals or his thunderbolts or anything." She turned back in time to hear the office lady cautioning Athena.

"Brace yourself for a shock," said Ms. Hydra's grumpy-looking green head. "You'll recall that your dad's office used to be messy before your stepmom got him to clean it up? Well, it's back to a disaster in there. Like a tornado hit it. Messiest guy I know," the head grumbled under its breath.

"Thanks for the warning," Athena told her cheerily.

When they entered Zeus's office, Hecate gasped. He was lying in the middle of the floor on his back, exercising. As in lifting an entire file cabinet with both hands! His muscled arms bulged as he heaved it up and down like it weighed nothing at all!

His office did kind of look like a tornado had struck, Hecate decided. Papers, maps, an Olympusopoly board game, and half-empty bottles of Zeus Juice were scattered all around the floor. Scrolls and architectural models of temples were stacked haphazardly on shelves.

There were scorch marks everywhere, too, she noted with a shudder. On the walls and the chair cushions. Probably caused by the electricity that was always crackling off Zeus, or maybe caused by the giant thunderbolt she'd just spotted on the wall behind his desk. It hung there, proudly displayed at an angle. It, too, crackled with electricity. The thing had to be at least seven feet long!

Seeing the direction of her gaze, Athena leaned over and whispered, "That's his favorite bolt. The first one he ever used in battle, during the Titanomachy. You know, the war between us Olympians and the Titans? It used to be on display in one of his temples, but he moved it here to replace a finger painting he made of his horse, Pegasus. Hera, my stepmom, convinced him it was a good idea. He's, um, not much of an artist."

While Athena was speaking, Hecate noticed that the ghost animals weren't obeying her earlier instructions. Not at all! The dog had begun licking some spilled juice. The cat, ferret, and monkey had immediately positioned themselves atop the file cabinet Zeus was pumping, apparently enjoying the up-and-down ride. And the unicorn was trotting around, poking holes in pillows and chair cushions with its horn.

A broad grin crossed Zeus's face when he saw Athena. He tossed the file cabinet aside and jumped to his feet before it hit the floor with a crash! The animals riding it shot off in surprise, leaping in different directions to make mischief elsewhere.

"Theeny!" Zeus boomed. "My smartest, most favorite daughter in the whole wide world!" He moved toward Athena with both muscled arms outspread. Meanwhile, the raven tried to land on his head, but it flew off in surprise when it got zapped. Fortunately, Zeus didn't notice.

Electricity fizzled from his fingertips when he hugged Athena, but she didn't seem to mind at all. Hecate backed up a few steps, trying to avoid any stray zaps.

Still smiling, Zeus went to sit on the huge golden throne behind his desk. In that glorious seat, he seemed even more impressive! "And you brought your new little friend, Hecktotty."

"It's *Hecate*, Dad, same as our Spell-ology teacher's name, remember?" Athena corrected gently. She gave Hecate an apologetic look.

Just then, Hecate felt hot breath waft across the back of her neck. *Oh no! What is that?* Slowly she turned her head. Then she let out a little squeal. Because there was a new, ninth ghost animal hovering behind her. A winged dragon!

It was green and scaly, and about as tall as she was. "I didn't think dragons and unicorns were real," she whispered, backing away.

"What?" Zeus and Athena both asked her in surprise.

"Oh, um, nothing!" Hecate replied in a strangled voice. She watched in horror as the dragon trotted over and nudged the papers on Zeus's desk with its long green nose, leaving scorch marks. Then it quickly joined the other ghost animals. Curious about this new arrival, they temporarily stopped destroying things to greet it. Zeus and Athena were oblivious.

Still, the animals would likely soon grow more rambunctious. Hecate needed to get business done and then get Athena and herself and those animals out of here! They'd arrived here thinking that convincing Zeus to let her remain at the Academy might take some doing. However, when he caught sight of her newly glittering skin, he thundered out, "You've turned into a goddessgirl? Fantastic! You're just what I need."

"I am?" asked Hecate, taken aback. She and Athena exchanged bewildered glances.

"Yes! I've been looking for a goddessgirl of witchcraft. You're already a witch," Zeus noted, gesturing to the pointy black hat she wore. "Now you're a goddessgirl, too. Obviously, you're the best choice!" he proclaimed. "Talk about perfect timing. I knew there was something special about you right off!"

"You did?" said Hecate. That wasn't how she recalled his reaction to her during their first meeting. And special? Really? She couldn't even successfully ride a broom. Plus, she only excelled in one class at Hexwitch. He didn't know all that, though.

She clutched her papyrus necklace and whispered a fact to herself. "Zeus is the King of the Gods, Ruler of the Heavens, and principal of MOA." That had to mean he knew what he was doing, even if *she* didn't understand why he'd chosen her for this new position.

"So this changes things, right?" Athena asked her dad.

Zeus nodded. "Yes, this changes things."

"How?" asked Hecate, looking between the two. (And trying to ignore the dragon, which had come over to sniff around Zeus's huge thunderbolt.)

"Well, for one thing, you can stay on at MOA, new goddessgirl. Certainly until Ms. Hecate returns, and then we'll see," Zeus declared.

Hecate smiled big. "Really?"

He nodded again, then tapped his fingertips on his desk while studying her. "To remain immortal, you'll need to partake of ambrosia and nectar from now on. The food and drink of the gods."

"Okay," Hecate said, distracted again by the antics of the ghost animals. The raven had perched on the dragon's snout and was pecking at the large thunderbolt behind Zeus. The monkey, cat, and ferret had begun hopping from one piece of furniture to another, playing the don't-touch-the-floor game. The peacock and unicorn appeared to be arguing over which one was more beautiful. And the pig was rolling around in a puddle of goo on the floor.

Desperate to get these ghost animals out of here before they got her into trouble (and kicked out of

MOA before Ms. Hecate returned), Hecate edged closer to the exit door.

"Sounds good," she told Zeus frantically. "Ambrosia. Nectar. Staying here for now. Got it, thanks!" With that, she zipped out the door, past Ms. Hydra, and out into the hallway.

Athena followed. "Wow! You're in a rush all of a sudden," she exclaimed.

"Just excited about the good news that I get to stay on," Hecate mumbled. This whole new goddessgirl title felt exciting, but also like a weight had fallen on her shoulders. "What duties do you think your dad will expect me to do in my new job? I'm a bit worried I'm not the best choice, to tell you the truth. I mean, I haven't even been able to ace my broom-flying test!"

All nine ghost animals had followed them out, and

they appeared a little alarmed at this information. Did they think her more special than she really was too?

But Athena gave her a quick hug of reassurance. "Don't worry. Like Aphrodite said, you're one of us now. The other goddessgirls and I will help you figure things out as you go along."

"That's a relief," Hecate told her with a smile. And it really was.

The ghost animals trailed them all the way back upstairs. For some reason, Aphrodite, Persephone, and Artemis were waiting for the two of them in Aphrodite's dorm room . . . wearing blue-and-gold cheer uniforms!

"It's Saturday. We have cheer practice, remember?" Aphrodite announced.

"Oh! I forgot. I'll go change and be right back!" Athena started to run off, then paused to glance back at Hecate. "Tell them the good news!"

"News?" echoed Artemis, eyeing Hecate after Athena disappeared down the hall.

"Yeah, Zeus named me the goddessgirl of witchcraft," Hecate told them.

A wide smile crossed Persephone's face. "Yay, you!"

"Congrats!" said Artemis.

"I think this calls for a cheer!" declared Aphrodite.

The trio put their three heads together to whisper among themselves. When they broke apart, they called out a cheer and did a little dance routine they'd made up on the spot:

"Hecate's a goddessgirl.
Woo-hoo! Hooray!
Now she can stay here
At M . . . O . . . A!"

When they shook their poms and jumped up and down, Hecate smiled. "Thanks, you guys! You're sooo sweet! Not sure how long Zeus'll let me stay though."

"But at least till your grandmother gets back," Artemis said confidently.

"Grandmother?" Hecate echoed blankly. Then she gave a start. She'd momentarily forgotten about her lie. "Oh, yeah, Ms. Hecate. Sure, that *is* lucky." She liked these girls and dreaded when they'd eventually learn the truth. Not only had she lied, but she wasn't a stellar student and couldn't fly a broom. So how could she possibly be suited to the title Zeus had bestowed upon her?

Just then Athena, in uniform now, dashed in the door and shook the poms she was holding. "Ready!" she announced.

When Athena, Aphrodite, Artemis, and Per-

sephone started to head out, Hecate followed. "Can I come watch you guys practice?"

"No!" the four girls turned to reply at once.

"No?" she echoed, ducking her head back in surprise. Well, that was kind of mean. She'd thought these goddessgirls liked her!

"That wasn't what it sounded like," Persephone said gently, as if she'd read Hecate's mind. "It's only that we'd rather you spend the time we're gone writing more questions and answers. So we can play your game after we're done with practice. And all weekend. With new cards! How fun will that be?"

"*F. U. N.* Fun!" cheered the other three goddessgirls, shaking their poms.

Hecate's eyebrows went up. Whoa! They wanted to play *all* weekend? They must *really* like her game. She smiled with delight.

Aphrodite led Hecate back to her homework desk. "Here, I'll get you set up to work," she stated, starting to clear everything off it.

As Aphrodite got Hecate the supplies she'd need, the ghost animals grew rowdier, and more inquisitive, too. The dragon began snuffling through boxes of letters under Aphrodite's desk, scorching them with its hot breath. Hecate figured these had come from mortals asking for advice about romance and stuff like that. The dog, she noticed, was nibbling on one of the pink sandals tucked in the closet. Hecate sidled over and nudged it away.

The pig had begun rooting around in the closet too, sending neatly stowed fashion items this way and that. The cat and peacock were now warily regarding each other in some kind of standoff. The raven sat on the windowsill, staring outside and pecking at the glass now and then.

Meanwhile, the monkey was swinging from the room's chandelier, while the ferret sneaked under a bed pillow to nap. The unicorn was poking the dragon with its horn, causing the dragon to giggle and snort smoke. None were behaving badly, exactly. They were just being, well, animals!

As was bound to happen, their combined actions attracted the four MOA girls' notice. They misinterpreted the cause, however. Glancing up at the swinging chandelier, Persephone commented to Hecate, "Hmm, your newfound goddessgirl powers seem to be a bit out of control today."

"Don't worry," Artemis said. "Things will probably calm down for you after a while."

"I hope so," Aphrodite said, frowning at the mess in her closet. Hecate wondered if the mega-neat goddessgirl was having second thoughts about leaving her alone in here. She could hardly blame her if she was! She must think Hecate's inability to control her new "powers" might result in her room coming to resemble Zeus's office!

"Don't worry, you'll get the hang of it eventually," Athena assured Hecate. "I was a disaster at magic my first week or so at MOA. I remember I did some brainstorming one night that accidentally caused a bunch of my inventions to rain down on Earth. Not that you'll do anything so awful. I just meant—"

"It's okay. I get it," said Hecate, smiling to show she wasn't offended. Obviously, she needed to get these animals out of here. If they were cooped up too long, they'd make mischief whether she was with them or not. She looked around the room, then back at the four goddessgirls. "Are there benches outside where you practice?"

They nodded.

"Okay, here's an idea. I've been collecting facts since I was six years old, so I can practically do it in my sleep. I'll come with you guys, sit on a bench, and work on my game cards there," Hecate assured them. "I'll just peek at your practice now and then. Promise."

Bam! Just then, a tube of bright pink lip gloss fell to the floor and rolled across it. In a streak of glowing white, the ghost cat, which had knocked the tube over, leaped from the makeup tray on Aphrodite's spare desk to her bed.

"Great idea!" Aphrodite said quickly. After scooping up the lip gloss, she flung the door wide. "Let's

go, everyone!" So they all did—not just the five girls, but the nine ghost animals too!

Hecate stuffed papyrus and charcoal into her bag and grabbed her black witch hat before following the goddessgirls out to the MOA sports fields. Every now and then she glanced over her shoulder at the cat, dog, ferret, peacock, pig, monkey, raven, unicorn, and dragon trailing her. Some, but not all, of these animals had been in the pet cemetery last night, she recalled. Had Melinoe noticed they'd gone missing?

And what could they possibly want from her, anyway?

9

Popular

Once they reached the sports field, Hecate stayed true to her promise and worked earnestly to create new fact cards while sitting on a bench. Often she would pause to admire her four new friends' cheer moves, and applaud or shout encouragements. "You go, goddessgirls!" she'd call out. Being on a team seemed like a lot of fun. If she went here, could she try out for cheer?

Her mind went to the Broom Zoom team back at Hexwitch. If she wound up at MOA, she'd never get a chance to try out for that team. Not that she could right now, since she hadn't passed her flying test. But she looked forward to trying again, in hopes of earning her own broom. It would be disappointing to miss out.

A shout from downfield caught her attention. It had come from another group of goddessgirls. Because all wore winged sandals, they were running relay races without their feet ever touching the ground. The sandals sped them along several inches above the track. It wasn't the same as flying on a broom, but it did look like fun!

Another group of students was playing some kind of ball game nearby. Among them Hecate recognized the godboys Ares and Poseidon, and a snake-haired mortal girl named Medusa. Their ball didn't fly in a straight line, she observed in surprise. Instead it darted here and there, zigzagging to keep out of reach.

Meanwhile, the nine ghost animals appeared to be having a terrific time frolicking around the sports field. Students out there had no way of knowing when a ghost dragon and a ghost unicorn joined their game, one on each team. Occasionally the two of them caused someone to miss a ball by chasing it and knocking it away. Sports games around here were certainly entertaining!

Hecate's thoughts chased around and around like the animals on the field as she worked on her cards and watched various MOA students. Time seemed to fly by faster than the Broom Zoomers back home! Soon the goddessgirls' team practice was over and it was time for lunch.

In the cafeteria, she sat with the four goddessgirls and Pandora again. Many students stopped by their table to ask about her game. Apparently, word about it was spreading, and many were curious to try it. She passed around some of the new papyrus fact cards she'd made during cheer practice.

Once she'd finished eating, Hecate excused herself and left the goddessgirls' table to check on the ghost animals. They weren't flitting around the room as they usually did, and she worried they might be up to trouble somewhere. As she walked casually around the cafeteria searching for them, she noticed that many students had already begun to play her game while still eating.

Finally, to her relief, she found the ghost animals all snoozing in a far corner of the cafeteria, near the door to the kitchen. Their romp on the sports fields must have left them pooped! The dragon and unicorn had curled up side by side, and all the others had tucked themselves around and on top of those two. The raven had even perched on the end of the unicorn's horn, its head tucked into its feathers. They all actually looked kind of sweet snuggled together like this.

"There you are!" called a familiar voice, causing her to jump in surprise. Hecate looked from the raven to see that Pheme had found her. As usual, the orange-haired girl's words puffed in the air like clouds so all could read them.

Pheme grabbed Hecate's wrist and pulled her to sit at an empty table. There the goddessgirl of gossip whipped a blank textscroll, a pen, and a small bottle of ink out of the bag she carried. Leaning close, she announced, "I want to interview you!" It was practically a demand!

"Me? Why?" Hecate shook her head in bewilderment. "I'm honestly not all that interesting."

"Your *game* is, though," Pheme insisted. She gestured toward the growing number of students who were playing it right now in the cafeteria. "That's what readers will want to know about. So, tell me how you began writing facts, why you enjoy it, and stuff like that. Speedy quick, please. My article is due to *Teen Scrollazine* in one hour."

Figuring Pheme was overestimating everyone's interest in her game, Hecate tried to make her answer as brief as possible. "Well, I've always liked and collected facts. I share them with students at my school, Hexwitch. And on my way here to visit MOA, I left question-and-answer cards at all the crossroads I came to. Walking long distances can get boring, right? So I thought, why not give travelers an opportunity to learn something along the way?"

Pheme grinned at her, writing hastily. "Good answer. Readers will love it."

"You think?" asked Hecate, scrunching her nose doubtfully.

"You must not have heard," Pheme said. "Your game has already become mega-popular among dozens, maybe hundreds, of mortals on Earth—literally overnight. It's going viral!"

"W-what? Really?" Hecate said, both pleased and surprised.

Nodding again, Pheme scooted her chair even closer. "Yes, really. In some cases, mortals have begun to travel to various crossroads simply to hang out there and read your facts. They are clamoring for more!"

"More fact cards, you mean?" said Hecate.

"Mm-hm. Speaking of facts, what's the name of your game?" Pheme asked. "I want to be the first one to tell everybody. It would be horrible if someone else beat me to it!"

"Name? Oh. Um . . ." Hecate tried to quickly think of one, but nothing came to mind. "It doesn't have a name," she admitted. "Maybe it could be called Q-and-As, as in Questions and Answers? That's not very special, though. Any other ideas?"

Pheme tapped her pen against her cheek, thinking. "Well, some mortals who played it with you at one of the crossroads are calling the game Trivia," she said. "It's a word that means 'random bits of information.'"

Hecate laughed. "Sounds about right. But random information can be useful and fun to know."

"Sure, sure. So is it okay if I say in my article that Trivia is the official name?" suggested Pheme.

At Hecate's nod, Pheme wrote the name down, then set her scroll and pen aside. With a wave of her hand, she summoned a mortal boy who'd been waiting nearby. He sat at their table and began making a sketch of Hecate!

"It's for my article," Pheme explained. "Okay, let's play your game now. I've seen the cards—cute, by the way. Love your lettering. Still, I can't review your game in my article unless I have personal experience playing it, can I?"

"Guess not," said Hecate, pleased to have her lettering complimented. "Okay, here goes." She pulled two cards from the necklace she was wearing and read off a question: "'Clotho is a member of what group? One: the nine Muses, who inspire art, literature, and science. Two: the three Fates, who determine human destinies. Three: the three

Graces, who lend beauty, charm, and creativity to immortals.'"

"The Muses?" guessed the artist.

"No! The Fates! And Clotho's sisters are Lachesis and Atropos," added Pheme. She took the card from Hecate, checked her answer, and then pumped her fist. "Yes! Got it right."

Pheme was obviously proud of the breadth of her knowledge. By the time she'd correctly answered a few more of the cards, the artist had finished his sketch, given it to her, and headed off.

Hecate stood. "Well, I'd better get going. I need to go back to my table and take my dishes to the tray return."

Pheme grabbed her wrist. "No, let's keep playing," she urged. Wow, she seemed really hooked on the game!

"But don't you have to go write your article? I thought it was due in an hour," asked Hecate.

Pheme looked torn, but her desire to spread gossip—er, information—won out. She grabbed her materials and the sketch of Hecate, then rose and made a beeline for the exit. "Thanks!" she called back to Hecate over her shoulder, leaving cloud letters puffing in her wake.

On the way to the tray return, Hecate looked around the MOA cafeteria. Most of the students here seemed to be playing her game now, passing the papyrus cards from table to table. Even the artist had joined some godboys in playing it.

Meanwhile, her movements had drawn the ghost animals' attention, and all had awakened. Feeling refreshed and energetic, they were up to their old tricks. The ferret and cat had floated up to the ceiling and were busy blowing out the candles in the chandeliers. The dragon was using its hot breath to blow papers here and there and to mess up everyone's hair.

But students were so busy with her game that they hardly paid attention to the mayhem. That is, until the unicorn began using its horn to spear food off plates and move it to other plates, causing accusations of food stealing among the boys. Students also began to take notice when the monkey started untying their sandal straps while they sat, so that they'd trip when they stood and tried to walk. And when the dog and pig began butting their chairs, causing them to tip over.

Hecate was horrified by the ghost animals' behavior. Having no idea how to control it, she decided to leave them be and tried to sneak out of the cafeteria before they noticed. No such luck. By the time she'd

made it halfway up to the dorm, they'd found her again and followed her back to Aphrodite's room. They soon crowded inside with her and resumed napping. She figured they were probably tired again due to their busy lunch shenanigans!

The rest of the afternoon, Hecate sat at Aphrodite's desk, enjoying the quiet, and wrote a bunch more game cards. By dinnertime she had created several tall stacks of questions and answers. That was a lot, so she decided she'd tack any extras onto the signposts on her trip back to Hexwitch . . . after the ghost curse was lifted. Whenever that finally happened. *Hurry up, Ms. Hecate!*

"Need any more charcoal?" Aphrodite dropped in to ask her a bit later. She set a tray of dinner for Hecate on the desk.

"Thanks for the food! Didn't realize it had gotten

so late. I'm good with charcoal, though. Mine's . . . er . . . *everlasting*. It's got a magic spell on it, I think." Hecate showed her the piece she held, which was still the same size it had always been. "So, should I just eat what you brought and keep working?"

Aphrodite nodded. "That would be great!" Seeing the stacks of cards Hecate had made, she asked, "Can I borrow these? Everyone's been asking if you've made new ones."

"Oh, um, sure," said Hecate. She was a bit dismayed, though. She didn't really want to spend her entire time at MOA making cards! However, she ate and then got back to work, reminding herself to feel grateful that her fact-collection hobby was so well appreciated here. Unlike at Hexwitch!

10

Famous

*T**HUMP! THUMP! THUMP!***

The next morning, Hecate sat up in bed. What was that noise? It had come from outside Aphrodite's window. All the ghost animals perked up too, cocking their heads to listen. Her fear of them was pretty much gone by now, she realized. She didn't even flinch when the dragon yawned, flicking its long forked red tongue!

From the bed opposite, Aphrodite yawned too. "It's just a magic breeze. Must be a delivery," she mumbled sleepily. Then she turned over, burrowing deeper into her covers. "I can't be bothered. Need sleep. We played your game till late last night."

Thump! Thump! Thump!

Hecate pushed off her covers and tiptoed over to the window, walking right through the ghost animals as if they weren't even there. She'd noticed they seemed able to choose whether or not to trip mortals and immortals. Sometimes, like now, they'd allow you to pass right through them.

When she opened the window, a magic breeze blew in, carrying a new edition of *Teen Scrollazine*. *Bang!* The 'zine hit the floor. Then the breeze whooshed back outside.

"Thank you!" Hecate called after it. She shut the window and picked up the scrollazine.

She was about to set it on a shelf when she noticed the picture of her, and then the headline. Her eyes bugged out as she read it aloud: "'You've Got to Try Hecate's Trivia Game! It's the Newest Craze!'"

"Huh? I've already tried your game," Aphrodite reminded her. She yawned again, still looking and sounding half asleep.

"No! That's the headline on the front page of *Teen Scrollazine*!" said Hecate, her voice high-pitched with shock.

"What?" In a flurry of frothy pink nightgown, Aphrodite leaped out of bed and rushed over to see. She took charge of the scrollazine and began reading aloud from the article. "'If you haven't played

Trivia yet, you are missing out! Hecate—who Zeus has recently named the goddessgirl of witchcraft—created this new game. Everyone's talking about it. Both immortals and mortals are playing it. Collect the game cards today!'"

Aphrodite's jaw dropped and she shot Hecate a thrilled smile. "Wow! Pheme's article about you covers the *whole front page*. It practically reads like an *ad* for your game! You're famous!"

"No, I'm not," Hecate said modestly.

"You soon will be," Aphrodite predicted. "Because everybody reads the 'zine."

Just then a quick knock came at the door. Persephone and Athena burst in, already dressed for the day. Athena was holding a copy of *Teen Scrollazine* too. Another girl, with long fire-gold hair, came in behind them. Hecate didn't know her. She'd

expected to see Artemis and Pandora with the others, but Artemis was probably out walking her dogs, since Hecate couldn't hear them barking next door. And maybe Pandora was sleeping in, since it was Sunday.

The open doorway seemed to spur the nine ghost animals to action. They streamed through it, even though they could have exited through the closed door and walls anytime they chose. As long as the door stayed open, however, they didn't seem to mind not being glued to Hecate's side. They floated off down the hall, looking for trouble, no doubt.

"Woo-hoo!" shouted Persephone, doing happy wiggle fingers. "Did you see it? Pheme's article?"

"It's huge! How could we possibly miss it?" said Aphrodite. Holding the 'zine so her two friends could read along, she settled in to read the entire article out loud.

These girls were more excited about the article than *she* was! Hecate decided. It was nice that people liked her game, but she didn't really care about becoming famous.

While Aphrodite was still reading the article aloud, the girl with fire-gold hair sidled over to Hecate. "Hi, I'm Cassandra. My family owns the Oracle-O Bakery and Scrollbooks shop in the Immortal Marketplace. Have you heard of it?"

"Ooh, yes! Your shop has the *best* cupcakes!" Hecate enthused, bouncing on her toes. "The cafeteria at my school down on Earth orders them for us for extra-special events."

Cassandra smiled. "Glad you like them." After a moment's hesitation, she said, "Persephone and Athena have been telling me how much fun your game is, and that gave me an idea."

Hecate raised an eyebrow. "An idea?" she repeated.

"Well, more of a proposition, really," Cassandra said.

"Oh?" Hecate looked at her a little warily, wondering what the proposition could be.

Coming straight out with it, Cassandra asked, "I was wondering if it would be okay if I put some of your papyrus game cards—instead of the usual fortunes—in batches of our bakery's Oracle-O fortune cookies. They'd be special batches to sell in our shop this week only. Sort of a promotional tie-in with Pheme's article."

Overhearing Cassandra's proposition, Athena clapped her hands. "What an awesome idea! I bet those special cookies would sell out fast."

"Especially since you're now a goddessgirl, Hecate," Persephone broke in.

"True," added Aphrodite, looking over. "Everyone will be very interested in you after reading this." She and Athena were sitting cross-legged on Aphrodite's bed now, while Aphrodite finished reading the article to them. Unseen, the ghost cat and ghost ferret had returned to the room and jumped up to cuddle around them. She was glad the dog hadn't joined them. Aphrodite would certainly be displeased if she got a whiff of dog breath.

What these girls were saying was very nice, Hecate knew. But writing a ton of game cards was turning out to be a lot of work. She pointed to the stack she'd made last night. "I have these done. But how many more would I have to come up with?" She wasn't at all sure she could supply enough for Cassandra's cookies, plus a bunch more for her game, if it got even more popular. "Oh, wait." She snapped her fingers and glanced at Aphrodite. "What about the cards I gave you last night? How many of those are left?"

"Um, none?" Pandora answered, having joined them at some point.

Aphrodite nodded. "She's right. Last night, girls up and down our dorm hall were playing. Some of them kept your cards to share with godboys and other friends."

As the goddessgirls went back to reading Pheme's article, Hecate gulped. All those cards were gone already? She was going to have to find a faster way to make more if this kept up.

"Speaking of ideas, where did you get the idea for your game?" Cassandra asked Hecate. "It's probably in Pheme's article, but since we've been talking while the girls are reading it, I didn't hear."

So Hecate began telling her about her fascination with facts. It was the same story she'd told Pheme, only now she added details she hadn't mentioned to the goddessgirl of gossip. "It was this girl I met on a field trip to an old cemetery who suggested I create a game from my facts," she mentioned to Cassandra after a while. "Her name was Melinoe, and—"

Hearing this name, Cassandra shot her a look of alarm. "Melinoe? But you're the goddessgirl of witchcraft, you say? Not of anything else?"

"Just witchcraft. Why?" Hecate asked, cocking her head.

"Oh, no reason," Cassandra replied quickly.

Aphrodite had finished reading the article aloud by now. Having overheard this last bit of conversation between the two of them, she went up to

Cassandra and gently nudged her. "No, there's something. C'mon. Give."

Cassandra shrugged. "It's just that, well, I met Melinoe myself a week or so ago. She came to our shop and wanted me to tell her fortune. I mean an *opposite* fortune, of course." She eyed Hecate, looking as if she was bursting to say more.

"An opposite fortune?" Hecate echoed. Athena spoke at the same time, so no one heard her.

"Is there something you're not telling us about this Melinoe person?" Athena asked Cassandra.

Cassandra twirled a strand of her fire-gold hair around her finger and then sighed. "I cannot reveal a fortune I've privately supplied to another. It wouldn't be fair. However, I *can* tell you she got really mad about what I revealed to her."

She glanced over at Hecate worriedly. "I believe Melinoe is someone to be wary of. Be careful of her. She might mean you harm. In fact, maybe I shouldn't draw more attention to you after all."

Yikes. Really? Hecate wished Cassandra could say more about the fortune she'd revealed to Melinoe. What could've made that ghost-animal girl so mad?

"Oh no! You're not going to back out of putting Hecate's game cards in your cookies just because of that Melinoe girl, are you?" asked Pandora. She'd been sitting at Aphrodite's spare desk, sniffing one of her perfumes. Now that she looked up, the dragon, who'd just returned, took the opportunity to sniff it over her shoulder. Unknown to her and the others, it then squinched its nose and sneezed, apparently not appreciating the unfamiliar smell.

"Yeah, those special cookies are such a great idea," Persephone agreed, sounding really disappointed.

"I don't know," Cassandra replied, twisting her hands together. "I'm just not sure it's the right thing to do." Her gaze fell on the stacks of cards Hecate had made last night. "Are these the famous cards? I haven't actually played the game yet."

Persephone's face brightened. "Oh, then you must play. It's sooo fun!" Even though it was time to go downstairs for breakfast, she grabbed the stack of cards, and the girls (all except Hecate) became involved in a game.

Cassandra was caught up in it in minutes and soon declared that she loved Trivia. "It's settled. You absolutely *must* make some cards for our bakery!" she told Hecate.

Hecate wrinkled her forehead. "But what about Melinoe? I thought you were worried that cards in your cookies might draw more attention to—"

"Oh, who cares about her!" Cassandra said, waving a hand in the air. "If she'd meant you harm she wouldn't have given you the idea for what to do with all those facts you collect, right?" Then she begged Hecate to spend the rest of the day in Aphrodite's room making additional cards. The other girls added their pleas as well.

Hecate was relieved to hear that Cassandra had changed her mind and decided Melinoe wasn't really a threat after all. "Okay," she told the girls. "I'll stay here and make more cards." Then she added wistfully, "Though I kind of hate to miss out on hanging with you."

"You won't!" Aphrodite declared. "Because, after

breakfast, we'll all come back here and help you write them."

To this, Hecate happily agreed. "Yes! Let's do it!" After borrowing a fresh outfit from Aphrodite, she got dressed, and then they joined the others in the cafeteria. Once they'd eaten, the six girls (plus Artemis, who'd stopped by after walking her dogs) all went back upstairs to Aphrodite's room and got to work creating more cards. Fortunately, the ghost animals weren't bugging them. Since many girls left their doors open along the dorm hall on the weekend, the animals were wandering in and out to explore, unbeknownst to those girls!

"While you guys keep working, I'll take the cards that are finished." Cassandra decided after a while. "I'm sure Ms. Okto will let me use MOA's kitchen to make batches of Oracle-O cookies to leave here in

the cafeteria for students and teachers. Later, I can take any more new cards you make to my family's shop to include in Oracle-Os for our IM customers." After gathering up an armload of the Q&A cards, she left to do just that.

Meanwhile, Hecate and her team kept on with their task of coming up with new questions and answers. There was plenty of giggling every time it came to supplying the two incorrect answers for each question. Some of those they came up with were super-silly! For instance: Jason and the Argonauts stole what golden object from King Aeëtes—a fleece, some geese, or his niece? Also: What do immortals wear on their feet to travel—Zeus boots, winged sandals, or Achilles high heels? And: What did Medusa turn into when she once saw her own reflection—a rock-star, con-Crete, or stone?

They'd all agreed that only Hecate would do the actual card writing, because Pheme's article had especially mentioned how fancy her lettering looked. This, of course, delighted Hecate. With everyone helping and chatting together about this and that, it turned into a totally fun time!

After a while they took a break for lunch, trooping down to the cafeteria again. Although the ghost animals followed them, they soon peeled off to snort and sniff at the various smells.

Hecate spotted Zeus the minute they went in. He was sitting at a table, beaming while reading the new issue of *Teen Scrollazine*. The other girls went over to say hi. But since he made Hecate nervous, she took a different route toward the lunch line, in hopes of avoiding him.

"YOU! Come here!" Zeus boomed.

Hecate froze mid-step, then turned and sent him a weak grin. Since he was staring straight at her, she had no choice but to do as he commanded.

Once she stood before him, Zeus flicked his fingers at the article about her game. "Pheme says this game of yours is getting mortals talking together at crossroads. And that's helping them become friendlier." He stood, looming over her. His powerful, muscled arm reached out. When he clapped a big hand on her shoulder, a zap of electricity shivered over her.

She hunched her shoulders. *Scraggletwix!* Was he planning to fry her to smithereens?

No! To her surprise, he exclaimed, "Well done, Hecate! I like that they're learning facts about us immortals from your cards." He gestured to the article again, and she let out a relieved huff when his

hand retreated. "Feel free to add more facts about me in future cards too. Athena can help. She knows all about my amazing exploits."

Hecate and Athena shared a quick grin over this. Zeus *had* done many amazing things. And he wasn't shy about letting everyone know it!

Suddenly he straightened and raised his head to sniff the air with great interest. "Do I smell *cookies*?"

"Indeed you do!" Cassandra sang out. She carried a large basket as she came toward him from the kitchen. "This is my first batch of Trivia cookies. They include Hecate's fact cards instead of fortunes. I'm going to set them out here for students and teachers to enjoy."

After dropping the 'zine on the table, Zeus rubbed his hands together in anticipation, then nabbed a handful. "Yummy, thanks," he mumbled around

bites of cookie. He quickly grabbed more, stuffed them in his pockets, and headed out of the cafeteria.

Athena grinned at Hecate. "In case you didn't notice, my dad has a major sweet tooth."

"You should make that into one of your game facts. As in: What's Zeus's favorite snack—carrot sticks, nectaroni, or cookies?" Persephone suggested.

Hecate giggled and glanced at Athena. "You don't think he'd mind?"

"Not at all," Ms. Okto put in. The cafeteria lady had overheard as she brought out four more baskets of Cassandra's cookies. "It's no secret how much he loves sweets. He won't care how many people know!"

Phew! It was a relief that Zeus seemed happy about her game and was okay with Cassandra using her cards in cookies. Feeling energized by his approval, Hecate and the others stayed up late that

night creating more papyrus cards. This was even after Cassandra left for the Immortal Marketplace with a large basketful of them.

Monday morning all was quiet when Hecate woke, even though the sundial outside showed it was already ten o'clock on a school day. Since Aphrodite was still asleep, Hecate decided to take time to cast a simple spell to instantly wash and dry herself. And to simultaneously wash and dry her school uniform—while it was still on her! She hadn't planned on staying at MOA this long, so it was the only outfit she'd brought. And though Aphrodite had been generous in letting her borrow chitons, they didn't really share the same sense of style.

Her spell went like this:

"Wishy, washy, wish I were fresh and clean,
And my uniform perfectly pristine!"

Poof! It worked! That done, she tried to wake Aphrodite, but without success. After mumbling that she was still tired, that girl buried her head under the covers.

"Aren't you missing your classes?" Hecate asked her. But Aphrodite was asleep again and didn't reply.

Feeling hungry, Hecate left the room and went downstairs alone to find something to eat. Alone . . . unless you counted the ghost animals, which followed her practically everywhere!

When she reached the cafeteria, she found that most of the tables were full of students playing Trivia. *Why aren't they in class?* she wondered. Breakfast was already over, but snacks had been set out, so she grabbed a bowl of ambrosia flakes and milk and found an empty table. The animals went roaming, sniffing at this and that and basically checking every-

thing out, as usual. Once she'd finished eating, she tossed her trash and turned to leave.

"Hecate! Come here!" Zeus roared. He was seated at a table with some teachers. Mr. Cyclops, the Herology teacher here at MOA, was among them, easy to recognize because he only had one eyeball, smack in the middle of his forehead.

"We've been up all night eating Cassandra's cookies and playing your game," Zeus told her once she'd obediently gone to him.

"Oh. Is this a holiday?" she dared to ask.

"Yes! A *surprise* holiday," Zeus informed her. "I'm calling it Trivia Day in honor of your game. I'm suggesting that everyone play it all day long. In fact, our students will be graded on how many correct answers they get."

"We're okay with that!" a godboy called from a

nearby table. He was sitting next to Artemis, who waved to Hecate. She guessed he must be her twin, Apollo. Both had the same dark hair and eyes.

"You bet! Yay!" other game-players cheered from around the cafeteria, echoing Apollo. Though everyone seemed happy, they also looked rather tired. Had these students been up all night?

Zeus shooed Hecate with his hands. "GO! Write some more fact cards before we run out!" he ordered.

"O-okay," Hecate promised. However, as she headed back upstairs, she began to wonder if her game was causing things to get a little weird around here. MOA students didn't seem to talk much anymore outside of playing it together. And she hadn't noticed any of them doing schoolwork. Plus, Zeus had just canceled classes! Her game was using up everyone's time.

By now, the cookies Cassandra had taken to her shop must be making their way into the world. Were mortals experiencing the same effects? Hecate wondered. If enthusiasm for her game spread further, she wouldn't be able to write fast enough to satisfy game-players' needs.

Like most witches, Hecate could write equally well with either hand, but all her fingers were still cramping from overuse. She flexed her hands, trying to ease their soreness. *Hey, wait a minute!* she thought. *Why can't I just cast a spell on the charcoal to make it write by itself!* She should've thought of that before!

By the time she got back to the girls' dorm hall, Aphrodite had left a note saying she'd gone to Athena's room to play Trivia. The note went on to suggest that Hecate should continue making more cards, since everyone was sure to need additional

ones soon. Hecate let out a tired breath. But then she got busy.

She picked up her charcoal from the spare desk. Cupping it within her palms, she chanted softly to it:

"Do my lettering,
Please, charcoal.
Questions. Answers.
They're your goal!"

It worked! The card-creation process instantly became super-fast. While she dictated the words to go on the cards, the charcoal wrote them by itself in a style identical to hers. Perfect!

While she'd been working, she heard the ghost animals messing around behind her. They were misbehaving in order to get her attention. Did they

hope to befriend her? She turned to gaze at them. They stopped what they were doing and stared at her with hope in their eyes. What were they hoping for, exactly? Surely they didn't think they were going to become her . . . pets?

"Look, you should know I don't really like animals. Nothing personal. You kind of scare me, so . . ." At her words, they seemed to droop. If animals could sigh sadly, she had a feeling these would.

Okay, now she felt bad. For once she didn't just look at them—she *really* looked at them, one after another. And she noticed something she hadn't before. Their eyes held a hint of sadness. Their expressions were disappointed. Like she was somehow letting them down.

She spread her hands wide, feeling frustrated. "I don't know what you want, but I'm pretty sure

I can't help you. Melinoe knows how to take care of you. So you should probably go back to her and leave me alone," she told them as kindly as she knew how.

"Who are you talking to?" asked a voice. She turned around to see that Persephone had come into the room.

"Um, nobody," said Hecate. Until Ms. Hecate returned, she wasn't going to admit she'd brought animal trouble to the Academy, since Zeus would surely disapprove and still might send her home before she could be cured. "Just talking to myself."

Persephone eyed the desk where she'd been working. "Oh, okay. Well, before it gets too dark, I was wondering if I could have some of those cards?" she began. "I'm going down to the Underworld to visit Hades, and I want to show him the game. He's been working on dredging the lake in the pit of Tartarus. I'm sure he could use a break by now, and playing your game would be fun!"

"Sure, you can take these." Hecate handed Persephone a stack of the new cards. Then, trying her best to ignore the discouraged looks on the ghost animals' faces, she got back to work.

11
The Underworld

TUESDAY MORNING, ZEUS DECLARED ANOTHER holiday from "schoolwork schmoolwork" (as he now called it). When Hecate went downstairs for breakfast, she took a fresh roll of papyrus and her everlasting charcoal to work on more cards. She'd been inside the school for a while. So she veered away from the cafeteria, deciding to duck outside and get a breath of fresh air before eating. As usual, the

nine ghost animals followed along behind her.

Everywhere she looked, inside the Academy or out, teachers and students were enjoying her game. They'd already been playing it in the dorms, but now they were also doing so in the MOA courtyard and on the sports fields. When she finally set foot in the cafeteria, she saw that it was full of game-players too. No work was getting done. And no food was being prepared, because even Ms. Okto and the cafeteria ladies were all hunched over a small stack of cards at one of the tables. It was Trivia fever!

Good thing the snacks table was still well supplied. Turned out, Hecate would have to help herself to ambrosia chips and dip and a carton of nectar three times that day for meals. When she came down for dinner, anytime someone spoke to her, it was only to beg her to create more fact cards.

She had to make them without the help of friends now, because Aphrodite and the other goddessgirls had flaked out on her. They'd become so captivated by her game that they brushed aside her requests that they all get together to create the cards, like before. Though it was great that everyone was having fun, an uneasy feeling was growing in her. It wasn't healthy for them to be playing her game to the exclusion of everything else. Was it?

As Hecate finished her dinner, she watched a worried-looking grown-up goddess enter the cafeteria and hurry over to Zeus. She asked him a question, but when he only grunted a reply and went back to his game, the goddess then rushed to a table where Aphrodite, Athena, Artemis, Pandora, and Pheme sat poring over fact cards as well.

Hecate thought she heard her asking them some-

thing about Persephone, but the girls just waved their arms to shoo her away, as if she were a pesky fly. When the goddess's desperate gaze swept the room and caught Hecate staring, she zoomed over.

"Hello. You're Hecate, right? I'm Persephone's mom, Demeter. She told me about your Trivia necklaces," she said gesturing at the one Hecate wore today. "And I saw your picture in *Teen Scrollazine*."

"Yes, she told me about you, too," Hecate replied, standing to greet her.

"I have unsettling news," Demeter went on, wringing her hands. "Persephone is missing. She was supposed to come home last night, but she never did. Have you seen her?"

"Not today. But last night, she told me she was going to the Underworld," Hecate revealed, starting to worry too.

"She went there at night? Without telling me?" Demeter practically yelled. "Why?"

"Well, she, um, had something to show Hades," replied Hecate. "My game."

Demeter frowned at her, then stared around the cafeteria. "This is so strange. That game of yours seems to be taking over everything. Persephone's friends and Zeus are so absorbed in it, they won't talk to me."

This really *was* strange, Hecate thought. How could Persephone's BFFs be more interested in a game than in helping to find her? It didn't make sense!

Demeter's eyes came back to rest on Hecate, and she asked her urgently, "Would you be willing to help? The Underworld's a big place. Two of us could cover more ground searching for her."

"Me?" Hecate squeaked out. Instantly, her hand reached to stroke the necklace she wore like a security blanket. The Underworld was hugely scary, unless you were dead. Which she wasn't. No way did she want to go there. Yet if her game was causing a problem for Persephone, it was her responsibility to help. "S-sure. I—I'll help you," she made herself offer.

"Demeter!" It was the nine-headed Ms. Hydra from Zeus's office. Her sunny yellow head was calling out from where she sat one table over with several game-playing teachers. "Come play with us!" she invited in a happy voice. She held up one of the papyrus Trivia squares face out, so Persephone's mom could read it.

Demeter blinked at it and then took a step toward her. "Oh, well, okay." Suddenly, she seemed to be considering the idea!

"What? No! We need to go find Persephone, remember?" said Hecate. She practically had to drag Demeter away. She was beginning to think her game might be contagious. Like the flu or something. She couldn't let Persephone's mom become infected!

Once outside, Demeter came to her senses again. She led Hecate to a chariot in the courtyard pulled by two wheat-colored horses. The ghost animals had started to follow them, but at the last minute they simply sat on the Academy steps as if prepared to wait for Hecate's return. She couldn't help feeling relieved to escape their sad eyes and unspoken expectations—for a while, anyway.

Briskly, the chariot flew Demeter and Hecate over farms, fields, and lakes. Hecate grabbed onto her pointed hat just in time to stop it from blowing off, then quickly tightened its drawstring under her chin. She couldn't help thinking how wonderful it would be to possess a flying broom someday—a partner she could sail the skies with!

As they drew close to the River Styx, she was dismayed to see that the nine ghost animals had appeared on its bank. By means of some sort of ghost magic they'd followed her after all.

Charon, the old man who ferried the dead across the river from Earth to the Underworld, could obviously see them and was trying to coax them into making that trip. But the animals backed away from his ferry, refusing to cross, and only watched Hecate with sad but hopeful eyes. Again she wondered what they could possibly want of her.

Melinoe had said that once ghosts crossed over into the Underworld, they'd instantly transform into shades. Why these animals refused to cross was a mystery. They'd likely wind up in the Elysian Fields, the Underworld's most desirable neighborhood, where everyone feasted and played forever more. If only they could speak and explain, so she could understand.

Ten minutes later, the chariot set down on Underworld soil and they hopped out. Hecate gasped, because almost immediately, they encountered an enormous three-headed dog lying with its head on its front paws.

Gulp! "Is—is that . . . Cerberus?" she asked, pointing at him.

Demeter nodded. "Don't worry. He's harmless—unless you disobey one of Hades's rules. If that dog is here, it means Hades is probably close by. And Persephone as well, I hope."

Hecate eyed the dog warily as they passed, then

relaxed when he didn't bother them. From there, the two of them walked hurriedly, Persephone's mom leading the way. Before long, they came upon a field of tall plant stalks, each topped with star-shaped white flowers.

"It's asphodel, the favorite food of the dead," Demeter remarked, noting her interest.

Three shades in the field sat around a small bonfire encircled by stones. They murmured with their heads bent forward to gaze at something they each held.

"Strange," Demeter went on. "They should be harvesting the asphodel blossoms. But they've all stopped working."

Soon Hecate saw why that was so. "They're playing my game! They must've gotten their cards from Persephone. I remember she took some to give to Hades," she told Demeter.

Apparently the Trivia craze had spread to the Underworld now! And before Hecate could prevent it, those shades pulled Demeter in to play their game with them. Instantly, Persephone's mom fell under its spell.

"Come, you can play with us too!" one of the shades urged Hecate. But she wasn't even tempted. Which was kind of strange, now that she thought about it. Why was she the only one who could say no to playing?

No amount of tugging on Demeter's arm or pleading with her could pull her away from the game. Eventually, Hecate gave up. She wanted to get out of this place. But how could she without Demeter to fly her? Plus, she'd feel terrible leaving Persephone and her mom behind. Seemed it was up to her to find Persephone now. Then maybe together they could return and rescue her mom. Where was that goddessgirl, though?

Hecate turned in a circle, gazing out in every direction. Seeing a sign indicating that the entrance to the pit of Tartarus lay ahead, Hecate remembered something Persephone had said: that Hades was dredging the lake down there. Tartarus was known to be the deepest, and very worst, place in the Underworld. It was where the truly evil were basically jailed—including those who'd offended Zeus. Hecate definitely did not want to go there!

Suddenly, and without warning, a large black stallion rose up beyond the sign, coming from Tartarus. She'd seen drawings of stallions like that in *Teen Scrollazine*. Four of them, all belonging to Hades. He and Persephone must be coming her way! However, the stallion galloped past her, its single rider looking neither left nor right. The rider was a glowing girl. One whose hair was half black and half white. *Melinoe!*

Melinoe had claimed she only herded ghost animals to the bank of the River Styx, but didn't enter the Underworld itself. So why was she here now, on Hades's horse? What had she been up to in Tartarus?

Hecate had to get to the bottom of this mystery! Persephone (and maybe Hades, too) might be in some kind of trouble! So even though she didn't want to go anywhere near Tartarus, she summoned all her courage and began to walk in its direction.

In minutes she was through its entrance and on a path that spiraled downward along the inside of the pit that was Tartarus. She shivered and hugged herself—more from fear than from cold—as she walked over damp, stony ground through patches of thick mist. Clutching the necklace she wore, she chanted random facts in an effort to calm her anxiety. "The Roman name for Hades is Pluto. The Roman name for Zeus is Jupiter."

Deeper and deeper she went. All too soon she came upon a tall signpost with multiple location arrows pointing in various directions. The names were gloomy-sounding: Mound of Misery, Ditch of Despair, and River of Fire. Beyond the posts, she caught a glimpse of that enormous lake, churning with hot bubbling mud and fire. Now and then, moans and screams rose from it. Talk about scary!

"The River of Fire is one of the five rivers of the Underworld and the place where the most terribly evil shades are forever doomed to dwell," she recited in a trembling voice. Truly frightened, Hecate was about to turn back when she heard two voices coming from the direction of the lake. One sounded like Persephone!

Hecate rushed toward the voices. Sure enough, the goddessgirl was sitting on a stone bench at the edge of the lake beside a boy about her age. He had dark eyes and longish dark hair. Hades! She recognized him instantly from *Teen Scrollazine*.

"Persephone!" Hecate called, going closer.

Neither immortal looked up from what they were doing. *Oh no!* They were playing Trivia! Each held only three cards, but they were playing them over and over again.

Hecate ran over and shook their shoulders. When they shrugged her off, worry and fear clutched her stomach. "What's going on?" she wailed aloud.

"My plan is unfolding," Melinoe informed her. Hecate whipped around to see that the girl had left

Hades's horse somewhere out of sight and returned here on foot.

"Plan?" Hecate repeated in confusion.

Melinoe crept closer. "You'll notice that Persephone and Hades are hypnotized by your game. Like others, they're no longer interested in eating ambrosia or drinking nectar. As the days pass, their immortal powers will fade as they play on. Like all the other immortals under your game's spell, they'll grow old, and eventually die as mortals do."

"No!" Hecate eyed Melinoe fiercely. "I never intended anyone to become spellbound by my game. If you know a way to break this strange hold it has over everyone, you must do it!"

"Why would I, when things are working out so well for me?" Melinoe grinned her eerie grin and began to circle Hecate, chanting:

"Magic charcoal, curse her game.
Let it bring her stress and blame.
But let it bring me super fame,
So everyone will know my name!"

The chant jolted Hecate's memory. "You used that spell to put a curse on my charcoal in the cemetery, didn't you!" she blurted, recalling the bits of it she'd heard Melinoe mutter.

Melinoe grinned. "Good trick, huh? Afterward, when you used the charcoal to write your cards, it made your game more . . ."

"Irresistible," Hecate finished, as understanding bloomed in her. "That charcoal is what caused my trivia to become mega-popular? Because of your spell."

Melinoe shrugged. "Everyone likes to answer a question correctly, right? And to learn information. It

makes them feel good. And smart. Writing your facts with bespelled charcoal boosted that good feeling times one hundred. So they'll never want to stop playing."

"But why do this?" Hecate asked again, spreading her arms wide in confusion.

"Because Cassandra foretold that Zeus would choose you to become a goddessgirl far more powerful than me." Melinoe's eyes blazed with anger as she jerked her thumb at her chest. "I deserve to be the goddessgirl of ghosts. Not you. It's totally unfair!"

"Me?" Hecate exclaimed. "That was the fortune Cassandra told you? But Zeus named me the goddessgirl of witchcraft, not ghosts."

"Duh. You're both, even if he hasn't told you yet," said Melinoe with a roll of her eyes. "There's a reason *my* ghost animals have begun following you. Did you think I wouldn't notice them deserting me?"

"I didn't steal the title you want so badly *or* those ghost animals. I never wanted either of them," Hecate assured her.

Ignoring this, Melinoe let out a happy cackle. "It's amazing how well my spell has worked out. Your trip to MOA and your stay at the Academy have spread Trivia fever beyond what I could ever have imagined. You put both mortals and immortals under your game's spell. Even Zeus! In fact, your success has given me an idea to take my plan further!"

"What do you mean?" Hecate asked, backing away from the girl with growing horror.

Mischief flickered in Melinoe's black eyes as she followed. "While everyone is caught up in the game, I'm going to literally *steal* Zeus's thunder. His mighty thunderbolt, that is. The Titans claim it to be a powerful destroyer. Now that Zeus is caught up in the Trivia craze, his power will slowly dwindle, until he won't be fit to rule Mount Olympus. Then, with the help of his bolt, I'll take over." She cackled again, and the terrible sound echoed across the lake. "I mean, why settle for becoming a mere goddessgirl when I could *rule*?"

Grasping the enormity of Melinoe's plan, Hecate gasped. "And after immortals no longer rule, you're planning to destroy all the cards, aren't you? Then, under threat of being blasted by that bolt, mortals will have to do your bidding. Is that what you're up to?"

"Exactly," said Melinoe, smiling unpleasantly. "But there's one last thing to do before I claim that bolt. You'll need to be, er, *neutralized*." Her eyes narrowed and she edged closer. "I bet you haven't actually played the game yourself since the charcoal was bespelled. Am I right?"

Hecate thought fast. Melinoe was wrong, of course. Hecate *had* played the game, both with mortals she'd met on the way to MOA and with the goddessgirls in their dorm. Somehow, she was certain it would be a bad move to admit this, though. So instead she nodded. She touched the pentagram point for honesty on her uniform, thinking that surely such an untruth could be forgiven if it wound up helping save everyone in the end. Fingers crossed.

"Thought so! Well, it's time you started playing!" Melinoe pointed to Persephone and Hades. "Or I'll shove them off their bench into the River of Fire."

Hecate didn't really believe Melinoe was evil enough to do that. But, just in case, she did her bidding and went to sit beside the pair. Both welcomed her as she joined their game. Was she about to be caught up in Trivia fever too?

No! When Hades and Persephone shared their cards with her, she didn't feel the overwhelming magnetic pull everyone else seemed to. But to fool Melinoe, she pretended otherwise. Which worked!

Convinced that Hecate had fallen under her own game's spell at last, Melinoe raced back up the path that would take her away from Tartarus. Once she was out of sight, Hecate plucked the fact cards from Hades's and Persephone's hands. Before they could stop her, she threw all six cards into the fiery lake. *Pzzt!* As they fizzled up in smoke, the spell on the two of them broke.

Persephone blinked. "What's going on? Why am I sitting here?" Hades looked bewildered too.

"I'll explain on the way out of Tartarus," Hecate told them, leaping up. "We need to rescue Demeter. And then Zeus and everyone else!"

To their dismay, no matter Hades's strength, they were unable to wrench Demeter and the shades from the game's power. Left no choice but to give up for the moment, Hades whistled, calling up his chariot.

"I hate to leave my mom, but she'll be safe enough here while we fly to the Academy together to try to fix whatever's going on," Persephone decided at last.

Hecate nodded and pulled her hat's drawstring so it wouldn't blow away in the wind they'd surely encounter. Since night had fallen, she lit two torches from the flames of the shades' bonfire. "To help light our way back to Mount Olympus," she explained.

The three of them—Hades, Persephone, and Hecate—leaped inside Hades's chariot. Normally it was drawn by four black stallions, but Melinoe had stolen one, of course. Fortunately, the remaining

three horses were enough to carry the chariot up and out of the Underworld.

Soon they were zooming toward MOA under a cloudy sky. Along the way, Hecate explained to her companions all that had happened with Melinoe.

12
The Bolt

IT WASN'T LONG BEFORE HADES'S CHARIOT WAS swooping them all down to Mount Olympus Academy. Though the school was shrouded in darkness, its polished white stone gleamed softly under Hecate's torches, standing five stories tall and surrounded on all sides by Ionic columns.

As the chariot dipped lower, she noticed dozens of students and teachers gathered in small groups

below in the courtyard. They were playing her game by torchlight! "There weren't enough new cards for them to play this long," she told the others. "Which means they're using the same cards over and over like you guys were back in Tartarus."

"Look! Melinoe must be here," Hades called, pointing. Sure enough, his missing black stallion was grazing on some grass along one side of the courtyard.

"I don't see *her*, though," noted Persephone.

The minute they landed in the marble-tiled courtyard, Hecate's nine animal followers appeared at the bottom of the granite staircase like magic. Ghost magic! They chased after her as she dashed up the steps. At the top, she placed her two torches in the twin decorative holders, one on either side of the Academy's bronze front doors.

"Calm down," she scolded, smiling a bit as the animals barked, meowed, yipped, oinked, snorted, and pranced around her. She couldn't tell if they were happy to see her, relieved she was safely back, or feeling some other emotion entirely. Regardless, it made her feel kind of . . . needed. Which was weird, in a good way.

She pushed through the heavy bronze doors. Unfortunately, when she glanced back, she saw that Persephone and Hades were still down in the courtyard, surrounded by students and teachers. *Oh no!* Despite all they'd just gone through, it had taken mere seconds for them to get pulled into another Trivia game.

Argh! There wasn't time to deal with that now, though. First she had to find Melinoe and stop her troublemaking!

Followed closely by her feathered, scaly, hairy, and furry companions, Hecate darted inside the Academy, down the hall, and all the way to Zeus's office. He and another grown-up she didn't recognize were sitting in the middle of the floor playing—guess what—Trivia! *Double argh!*

Her eyes caught a flash of white light over by Zeus's desk. *Melinoe!* The glowing girl stood there, facing the wall behind his golden throne while reaching for his enormous prized thunderbolt.

Zap! An electric charge shot between it and the girl's fingers. She snatched back her hands, shaking them. "Ow! I need gloves," she muttered. When she spun around to search for some in the drawers of Zeus's desk, she spotted Hecate.

"You escaped?" Although startled, Melinoe quickly advanced on Hecate, putting on the too-big Zeus-size

gloves she'd found. "Never mind. I don't care. You can't stop me. So back off. Or else."

"Or else what?" Hecate asked defiantly. Was that *her* voice sounding so bold? And when had she started behaving fearlessly? She was embarrassed to realize that she hadn't even tried to resist Melinoe back at the River of Fire. If she had, she might've been able to shove her into that lake as Melinoe had threatened to do to Persephone and Hades. *No!* She knew she would never do something so awful, and doubted Melinoe would have either, if it came down to it. Still, Hecate did believe she'd steal Zeus's bolt if she could.

Oof! Ow! Before either girl could take another step closer to the other or say another word, both found themselves pushed from behind. On purpose or by accident (Hecate wasn't sure which), the ghost

animals had barreled into them. Melinoe tumbled head over heels, and Hecate fell to her knees, her hat toppling to the floor.

As Hecate righted herself, picked up her hat, and shoved it back on her head, irritation welled up in her. "Can I help you with something?" she asked the ghost animals through gritted teeth. "For Zeus's sake, tell me what you want already! Why do you keep following me?"

At once, smiles swept over the faces of all nine animals. "Finally, you've spoken the magic words!" the ghost unicorn informed her, doing a happy little prance. Words she could understand tumbled from each animal now, all anxious to explain.

"'Can I help?' That's the pea-perfect question we needed to hear!" the ghost peacock exclaimed. It shook its beautiful plumage, looking pleased with her.

"Yes! Seems like we've been waiting *ferret*ever—er, forever—for you to ask it so you could understand what we need!" exclaimed the ferret.

"The reason me-*ow* and the others have refused to enter the Underworld is because there's something each of us has left undone," said the cat.

"Righty-*oink*! First we must each fulfill one last wish here on Earth," said the pig.

"*Ooh! Ooh! Ah! Ah!* And after that, we'll quit monkeying around," added the monkey.

"So that's why you've been following me? Because you think I can grant your wishes?" asked Hecate, shaking her head. "Why would you think I could do that?"

Melinoe, who'd risen to stand again, had been glancing back and forth between Hecate and the animals. Now she frowned, asking, "You can understand them—the ghost animals?"

Hecate nodded. "Not till now, though. Something's changed."

Melinoe stomped her foot in outrage. "How come you can, but I can't? It's not fair!" She looked a bit hurt, as well as angry. Like she was feeling left out.

"What changed is that you *finally* asked us the doggone right question," the dog told Hecate.

"And *caw-caw*-'cause you were ready to hear our answers," said the raven.

"Melinoe will never understand us. It just isn't meant to be," said the dragon. Glancing at that girl, it huffed a sad puff of green smoke from its nostrils.

Melinoe huffed back at it (without the green smoke), then spoke to Hecate. "What did that dragon just say?" Without giving Hecate a chance to answer, she went on quickly. "Never mind. Again you outdo

me! But I will defeat you in the end!" She headed for the thunderbolt once more.

Hecate hurried after her. "I'm not trying to outdo you! Honest!"

Suddenly all the animals began to speak to her at once. It was loud and confusing. But the basic gist was, "Wait! We have more to say!"

Hecate called back to them over her shoulder, "Okay, copy that. But can I get back to you on your requests later?"

Meanwhile, a determined glove-wearing Melinoe stood behind Zeus's throne, prying at his bolt once more. *Creak!* It began to budge! Was her dastardly plan going to succeed after all? That would be disastrous for Mount Olympus and all of Earth!

As in past anxious moments, Hecate abruptly found herself blurting facts. "Mr. Cyclops's

brothers—Brontes, Steropes, and Arges—make Zeus's thunderbolts. They're charged with electricity. Basically indestructible. Best used only by an expert like him."

"Whatever! I'm not worried," scoffed Melinoe.

"Don't!" Hecate warned. "Touch that bolt the wrong way and it could fry you, even through those gloves!"

Still, Melinoe ignored her. *If only I were brave enough to stop her!* thought Hecate. Instead she wanted nothing more than to run away. She eyed the office door. She even took a step in that direction. Then she froze as an idea came into her mind. It was the charcoal that had caused all the trouble, right? She reached into her pocket and felt it there.

What would happen if she destroyed it? Would the game's spell end? Would Zeus snap out of his

daze and stop Melinoe himself? She pulled out the charcoal, threw it to the floor, and stomped on it. *Scraggletwix!* Nothing happened. She picked it up and saw it had no cracks in it at all. Was it uncrushable?

It would be safest to escape before Melinoe claimed Zeus's thunderbolt. *No!* Hecate took a deep breath for courage. "There are scary things in the world. That's just a fact of life," she murmured to herself. "Now that I'm the goddess of witchcraft (and maybe of ghost animals too?), I have to learn to deal with them."

Just then, the dragon patted her shoulder with a clawed hand, as if trying to boost her courage. Out of nowhere, a new idea hit her.

"Dragon," she whispered. "Burn this charcoal to ashes, and I promise I'll do my best to help you animals get your last wishes!"

She tossed the piece of charcoal high in the air. Then she dropped to the floor and curled into ball, peeking out from under one arm. She might have been feeling braver, but she was totally not ready to get fried by dragon flames if they flared out of control!

Zzzt! Fire shot from the ghost dragon's snout, its aim true. *Poof!* In midair the charcoal fizzled away to nothing. *Hooray!* Though it couldn't be crushed, it apparently *could* be burned up by dragon fire! That hot stream of breath had also scorched a far wall. But, hey, what was one more scorch mark in an office already full of them?

Instantly, Zeus dropped the cards he'd been holding and glanced around his office in confusion. His gaze sharpened when he spied Melinoe. Although the girl had watched the charcoal's destruction, she was nevertheless still trying to steal his thunderbolt. Electricity began to crackle over Zeus's arms. His piercing blue eyes blazed with anger, and he leaped to his feet. "Who are you, and what do you think you're doing?" he roared.

Caught in the act, Melinoe whipped to face him. "Who, me? Actually, I was using these gloves to straighten your thunderbolt for you. All straight now. So I guess I'll just be going." She stripped off the gloves and headed for the door, obviously planning to escape. But Zeus blocked her way.

Hecate sprang to stand where Zeus could see her. "Not true! She was trying to *steal* your bolt!" She quickly explained to him all about the hexed charcoal and Melinoe's plot to rule Mount Olympus. Zeus's anger grew as he listened.

"Nuh-uh!" Melinoe yelled at her. Her voice was

edged with fear, though. Fear of what Zeus might do to punish her!

Before anyone else could speak, Persephone and Hades dashed in. Immediately Persephone noticed the grown-up who'd been playing cards with Zeus, and called, "Ms. Hecate! You're back!"

Pheme burst into the office right behind the pair, excitement on her face. "The Trivia game trend is suddenly fading! You heard it from me first!"

"Oh, great, just great," Melinoe fumed under her breath. "Destroying the charcoal must've released *everyone* from the game's spell. Which means all my efforts have gained me nothing!"

But Hecate was still stuck on what Persephone had said. "*You're* Ms. Hecate?" she asked the woman who now stood by Zeus. The woman—er, teacher—nodded, still looking a bit dazed.

"I came to see you a few days ago, but you weren't here," Hecate went on excitedly. "I was going to ask you to remove a curse from me. But I guess there never actually was a curse on me." In fact the glitter hadn't been a curse, nor had the ghost animals, she realized right then. Ms. Malediction's diagnosis had been wrong, but understandable in view of Hecate's symptoms.

The dazed expression left Ms. Hecate's face. "Yes, you're correct, though Melinoe did place a curse on your piece of charcoal. I saw her do it."

"You did?" Melinoe, Hecate, Zeus, Persephone, Hades, and Pheme said at the same time.

Ms. Hecate frowned at Melinoe and nodded again. "I watched everything that happened in the cemetery near Hexwitch School when you and Hecate met that night."

Turning back to Hecate, she went on as everyone listened in fascination. "I was there because your teacher Ms. Frogwart had written to me about you. She saw something special in you, so I came to determine your powers and offer you counsel. Before I could do any of that, however, you were tested by Melinoe."

"But if you knew what she'd done, why did you let all of this happen?" asked Hecate, spreading her arms wide. "Why didn't you stop her?" Speaking of stopping Melinoe, that girl was slowly trying to sneak her way to the door while Zeus's attention was on their conversation.

Ms. Hecate smiled kindly at Hecate. "I wanted to see how you would handle the problems she caused. However, although I knew she was up to something, I couldn't have known how bad things would get. That she would dare threaten Zeus's rule."

She paused, then went on. "You have the makings of a powerful goddess, Hecate. I came here to discuss your future with Zeus today, but am sorry to report that I became enthralled with your game myself."

At last, Zeus noticed Melinoe trying to ease past him. "Oh no, you don't!" he boomed, blocking her way once more. "What were you thinking, trying to steal my bolt? Even if you possessed it, did you really believe *you* could do *my* job?"

She flinched, her dark eyes apprehensive.

"It's not that easy, trust me," he went on. Hecate had a feeling he was speaking to everyone in the room, not just Melinoe, as he added, "Overseeing everything and everyone on both Mount Olympus and Earth is challenging! Problems everywhere, always needing my attention. I love my job, though, and no one could do it better, if I do say so myself. And I do!" He pounded one meaty fist into the palm of his other hand and glared at Melinoe. "Now, explain your actions!"

From the moment the game's spell had broken, the ghost animals had gone quiet and still. Currently, they stood, perched, or sat, with their heads turning back and forth to watch and listen. Which was pretty much what the immortals in the room who weren't involved in the conversation were doing too.

"I was jealous of her, okay?" Melinoe confessed, gesturing to indicate Hecate. "Cassandra foretold that I'll always be in her shadow. Why should Hecate get to be the goddess of witchcraft *and* ghosts while I remain a daemon in charge of nothing? It's not fair!"

"Ghosts?" Pheme echoed. Her expression had sharpened with interest, Hecate saw. Now that the goddessgirl of gossip was listening, any secrets spoken here would soon get out!

If Melinoe had hoped her little speech would get Zeus to go easy on her, it didn't work. His bushy red eyebrows rammed together in anger. Pointing a finger at her, he bellowed, "Stop with your talk of ghosts! The real issue here is your despicable curse on that charcoal. It could've wound up causing immortals to weaken—even die! On top of that, you dare try to steal my thunderbolt and usurp my power? For these crimes, I hereby banish you to Tartarus!"

Whoa. Tartarus? Although Hecate understood that Melinoe deserved punishment, it would be a shame if her abilities weren't put to good use. Just then, something sharp poked her in the arm. "Ow!" She jumped around to see that the unicorn had intentionally bumped her with its horn.

"Hey! What about us?" it asked her, pointing its horn toward the other ghost animals.

"I promised to help you and I will. Just please wait till we're out of here," Hecate told them.

"Who are you talking to?" Zeus demanded from behind her.

Hecate turned back to see all the immortals in the room looking at her strangely. Her cheeks turned pink with embarrassment. Time to fess up. "Um, well, speaking of those ghosts Melinoe mentioned? They exist. They're who I was talking to just now."

Though startled, no one appeared frightened by this news. Because, of course, immortals encountered strange and wondrous things all the time!

As fast as she could, Hecate explained how the ghost animals from the pet cemetery had come to follow her and why. "There are nine of them in this room right now, and they've asked for my help in fulfilling their final wishes, which I'm willing to do, if allowed."

"Hmm," said Zeus. He tapped his big chin, as if deep in thought. Suddenly his eyes lit up. Turning to address everyone in the room, he announced in a booming voice, "I do allow it. And I hereby declare Hecate to be the goddessgirl of both witches *and* ghosts! Ghosts of the animal kind, that is."

To Hecate he said, "Henceforth you will help to fulfill any ghost animals' last wishes here on Mount Olympus and on Earth, before seeing them to the Underworld."

Hecate gasped. It was official, then. But, again, the weight of *two* new jobs felt too heavy for one person.

"See how quickly I came to my decision?" Zeus

said to Melinoe. "That's what great leaders like me can do!"

"Like I said before . . . no fair!" sulked Melinoe.

Before Zeus could explode and use his quick decision-making skills to blast the incorrigible girl to smithereens, Hecate surprised everyone in the room—including herself—by speaking up on Melinoe's behalf.

"Wait! Melinoe's sort of right," she blurted. "Out of kindness, she was the first to take on the job of herding ghosts. I'm starting to like these animals and want to help them too. But it's a big job. Seems only *fair* that she and I share it. Maybe after I lead the ghost animals across the River Styx, she could take over herding them into the Underworld, where they'll become shades. Melinoe once told me she thinks the Underworld is amazing, but it actually scares me."

At her suggestion, Melinoe nodded eagerly. Most of the ghost animals nodded too, seeming to approve of Hecate's idea.

Persephone raised an eyebrow. "After all Melinoe did, you're sticking up for her?"

Hecate shrugged. "Yeah, I guess I sort of am. I know what it's like to yearn to be truly good at something and to be recognized for that skill," she said, thinking of her failed broom tests. "And Melinoe *is* good at her job. The ghost animals behave much better for her than for me. Over time, maybe we can learn from each other how best to do our jobs."

Hecate eyed Melinoe. "You're sorry for all the trouble you caused, aren't you?"

Melinoe twirled a finger in her hair. There wasn't

a shred of regret in her voice as she answered, "If you say so."

Hecate gritted her teeth. What was wrong with this girl? Didn't she realize she was trying to help her?

Zeus glared at Melinoe. "I don't think you appreciate how nice it is of Hecate to speak on your behalf. Well, since you seem to like games that involve picking one of three choices so much, let's try this. I'll give you three options to choose from, and you pick the one you like best."

He held up a finger. "One: I can fry you to smithereens right now." He held up two fingers. "Two: I can lock you up in Tartarus's fiery pit forever. Or, three," he said, holding up three fingers, "you can apologize to Hecate, accept her job-sharing offer, and go dwell in the Underworld."

"I choose number three!" Melinoe replied hastily. She turned to Hecate. "I apologize."

Then she turned back to Zeus. Pressing her luck, as usual, she said, "I'll need a title. How about Animal Herder of the Underworld?"

To everyone's surprise, Zeus just rolled his eyes. "Sure. Whatever."

"Goody!" Melinoe shouted, clapping and bouncing on her toes. "I'll be the best Animal Herder of the Underworld ever. You'll see."

Zeus narrowed his eyes at her. "I suggest you get going!" he growled. "Before I change my mind."

This time Melinoe had the good sense not to provoke him. She waved to the ghost animals in farewell, calling, "I'll see you in the Underworld when you're ready!" Then she darted out of the room, her black-and-white hair flying out behind her.

Minutes later, Hades and Persephone left for his chariot, planning to return to the Underworld, where they'd make sure Demeter got to her own chariot safely. Just when Hecate thought all was settled and she could leave the office too, Ms. Hecate spoke up. "So! I hear you're my granddaughter."

Zeus did a double take. "You mean she's not?" He was frowning as he looked from Ms. Hecate to Hecate.

Uh-oh, thought Hecate. Her shoulders hunched in embarrassment. "No, I'm sorry. I lied about that." *What will happen now?* she wondered. Would Zeus take back the titles he'd just given her? Would he thunder-blast her, as she'd feared all along?

Speaking to Zeus, Ms. Hecate said, "No, I'm not her grandmother. However, I have taken an interest in her abilities."

To Hecate the teacher said, "It sounds as though you may look to Melinoe for guidance in your work with the ghost animals. I'd like to help guide your talent as the new goddessgirl of witches, if we can find a regular time to meet."

"Really?" Hecate said, hugging both hands to her chest in delight. "That would be awesome!"

Zeus folded his muscled arms over his chest, looking at Hecate with a displeased expression. "Still, lying is unacceptable."

Ms. Hecate raised an eyebrow in his direction. "In view of how she's helped everyone here, including you, I think one small lie can be forgiven, yes?"

Zeus nodded a few seconds later. "Agreed. Forgiven. But only this once." To Hecate he said, "And I'll expect you to explain and apologize for your lie to anyone who might be aware of your false claim."

Hecate bobbed her head, knowing that this was, well, *fair*. It was a relief to have the truth out and things settled. And even though Ms. Hecate wasn't her grandmother, it was thrilling to find out that she wanted to work with her!

"One last thing," Zeus announced in a formal tone. "As befitting your new status as goddessgirl of witches and ghosts, I hereby officially invite you to attend Mount Olympus Academy." His intense blue eyes fastened on Hecate's black ones. "The choice is yours to make. Tell me, would you rather enroll here, or remain at your old school?"

Hecate straightened in pleased surprise. It seemed she had come to a new crossroads. Which way should she go? Down the path that would bring her to this school, where her new goddessgirl friends and Ms. Hecate would be around to help her learn more

about her goddess and witch powers? Or should she choose the more familiar path and remain at her old school, with her best friends, where she could also hone her witchcraft skills?

Stay at Mount Olympus Academy? Or return to Hexwitch School?

MOA or Hexwitch?

It was a hard choice. And then it wasn't.

"I choose both," Hecate told Zeus, her voice full of confidence.

13

Broomie

IT WAS TUESDAY, JUST A WEEK SINCE THE showdown with Melinoe in Zeus's office. Hecate was at Hexwitch today, outdoors in Broomstick Studies. Zeus had agreed to her request to attend both MOA and Hexwitch, as long as she could keep her grades up. And she was trying, spending more time on schoolwork rather than always focusing on her facts.

On her new schedule, she spent Mondays and

Tuesdays at Hexwitch School, and Wednesdays and Thursdays at MOA. Fridays were spent helping ghost animals make their final, dearest wishes come true. As it turned out, it wasn't just a duty. It was an occupation that truly satisfied her. Animals weren't so bad (or scary) after all, once you got to know them.

Although the Trivia trend had ended, and her game would never be quite as popular as it once was, both mortals and immortals still enjoyed playing it. But only occasionally, and not with the feverish delight from before. So she still wrote new questions and answers for the game from time to time, using regular, un-bespelled charcoal.

Strangely, no one at Hexwitch had come under her game's thrall, even though many students and teachers had played it. It seemed that, for reasons

unknown, witches, including Hecate, were immune to the hypnotic effects of the game. Good thing!

"Ready, Hecate?" asked Ms. Zoomly.

Hecate gave a thumbs-up to her Broomstick Studies teacher and turned to face another magic broomstick. For the thirteenth time, she was about to attempt a flying test. The broomstick hovered horizontally, several feet above the ground, about five yards away from her.

As happened with each test, she'd been given a new broom to try in hopes that the match might prove a satisfactory one. This particular broom had a bright red handle that matched the stripes in her leggings. Black hickory sticks had been tied together to form its sweeping end. For some reason, no one had yet been able to ride it successfully, though many had tried. So it seemed unlikely that she'd have better luck. Memories of her last disastrous attempt crept into her mind. *No!* She refused to let them crush her confidence.

Her teacher and classmates watched Hecate approach the broom. Jinx and Agatha smirked at her, no doubt hoping she'd fail. Ignoring them, she focused on the smiles and thumbs-up of her friends Willow, Hazel, and Poinsettia.

With one hand she reached to clasp the two necklaces she wore. Both were new. One was strung with small square pieces of papyrus upon which her Hexwitch friends had each written an encouragement. Things such as: *You've got this! Fly high! Rock it, Hecate!* Just thinking about what they'd written made her feel more sure of herself. And happy, too.

A magic breeze had brought her the other necklace only this morning. It was strung with similar

notes written by her new friends at Mount Olympus Academy:

Fly smart! You can do it, goddessgirl!

from Athena

Have a beautiful flight!

with love from Aphrodite

Sending you and your broom some flower power!

from Persephone

My dogs and I are cheering you on!

from Artemis

Let's get together for another interview after you ace your test!

from Pheme

What's it like to fly on a broom?

from the curious Pandora

THUNDER ON!

from Zeus himself!

Hecate squared her shoulders and held her head high. She could . . . no, she *would* do this! She strode up to the broom and wrapped her fingers around its shaft. Calm determination filled her as she slung one leg over to straddle it.

"Hecate, meet Broomie," said Ms. Zoomly. "Broomie, meet Hecate," the teacher said to the broom. "As you know, both witch and broom must happily bond for a match to be successful. Each of you has been trying to find a good match for a long time. May luck be with you today." Ms. Zoomly smiled kindly at them both, then stepped away.

Hecate had watched others try to ride this broom before. None of them had lasted more than a couple of minutes before being tossed off. But, like her, maybe Broomie just hadn't yet found its right match?

"I think we're going to be good together,

Broomie," she told it, her tone sounding both friendly and upbeat. "So don't even think about bucking me off. Friends don't dump friends, right?"

It was time. Hecate pulled her pointy black hat's drawstring snug at her chin. Taking a deep breath, she patted the broom's handle. "This is my thirteenth flying test. Thirteen is a lucky number for witches, so c'mon, let's do this! Fly!"

In an instant they were off. *Whoosh!* The wind blew Hecate's long, wild, black hair behind her as they flew. Excitement rose in her. She focused on her goal—a perfect flight in the shape of a five-pointed pentagram.

"You can do it!" "Go, Hecate!" she heard classmates call from below.

Floating in nearby trees or just above the ground were ghost animals that only she could see and hear

as they cheered her on too. *Bark! Oink! Whinny! Yip! Squeak!*

There were only five of them now. They hung out playing with one another in the pet cemetery, except when she worked with them on Fridays. She'd already helped six of the original ones—the cat, ferret, peacock, monkey, raven, and dragon—pass over into the Underworld after making their wishes come true. Only the dog, pig, and unicorn were left. Plus two new ones—a hedgehog and a goose—that had recently come to her for help with their final wishes.

Speaking of five, maybe this time she'd make all five points in under five minutes to pass her flying test. Her confidence was shaken when the broom suddenly jerked right. She'd seen it do that to other witch-girls too, forcing them into a figure-eight pattern.

"No figure eights," she murmured firmly as she

tightened her grip on the broom. "As fun as that might be, let's get the *five*-pointed pentagram out of the way first."

She'd learned a little something about how to be both kind and firm since she'd begun working with the animals. Would it work? To her surprise, the broom obeyed her immediately.

"Thanks, I knew you could do it," Hecate told it. "After we ace this test together, we can try other stuff. But first I'll show you my room. I think you'll like it. You'll have your own closet. And a home with me forever. We'll be best buds. Broommates! Promise."

The ghost dog had excellent hearing. "You can trust her," it shouted up from below. "She's very helpful and honest. She keeps promises!"

It seemed her broom must have been able to hear the animals, because it calmed even further. Unlike

the last twelve brooms she'd test-flown, it didn't resist her again. They made the first two of the pentagram points. She hung on, her arms and knees tight—but not too tight—around it. Before she knew it, they'd executed a flawless pentagram in the air in less than the allotted time. Then, *whoosh*! They dove down for a perfect landing!

Before she hopped off, she gave the broom a hug. "We did it, Broomie!" she whispered, hoping it was as pleased as she was. It must have been, because it curved itself into a big smile shape before snapping straight up again.

"Was that a smile, Broomie?" she asked. Its tip nodded, and she giggled.

Ms. Zoomly overheard. She beamed at Hecate. "Congratulations! That was a solid pass. Nice work,

Hecate and Broomie. You are officially now a forever team."

Hecate wrapped her arms around her broom and hugged it again. "Thank you, forever friend. You won't regret choosing me. I promise to be a good witch partner."

The school Broom Zoom team had begun its practice overhead with a fantastic loop-de-loop. Hecate stayed to watch as the group flew in formation and landed together with precision on the grass.

"Maybe we'll be that good someday," Hecate whispered to Broomie. It bent the tip of its handle in another nod.

"You and your new broom should try out," said a voice.

Hecate looked around to see that one of the

Broom Zoomers was speaking to her. "Me? Us? For the flying team, you mean?"

The witch-girl nodded. "I know you only just passed your test. But that pentagram you did was spot-on perfect. You made it look easy. And it's not."

Hecate felt her cheeks color with pleasure. "You were watching? Thanks. Couldn't have done it without my new buddy, though." She patted her new broom.

"Well, keep practicing together," the girl told her. "I think you guys have potential!"

"Thanks, we will!" Hecate smiled at the witch-girl as they parted.

Tomorrow she and Broomie would fly to Mount Olympus, since Wednesday was an MOA school day for her.

She loved being able to go to both MOA and Hexwitch, but weekends were the absolute best. Because that was when she got to hang out with friends from one or both schools. She had lots of friends now. Yet maybe her best friend would turn out to be this new broom!

With Broomie, it would be a cinch to fly speedy-quick between MOA and Hexwitch. As a part-time student at both schools, she would learn to excel as both a goddess and a witch. How amazing was that!

"We'll keep working on our skills until we're ready for Broom Zoom team tryouts. I know we can do it . . . together," she told her forever broom.

She surprised herself at how confident she sounded and felt. After daring to stand up to Melinoe and braving the Underworld, she was sooo over being scared of everything. She wasn't sure if they'd make the team or not. But she would try her best. She had a good feeling about it.

And that was a fact!

Authors' Note

Hecate (HEH-kah-tee or HEH-ket) is the Greek goddess of witchcraft, ghosts, and crossroads. Ancient Greeks left small gifts for her at crossroads—the intersection of two or more roads. Often, these travelers would share news with others they happened to meet there. This led to the spreading of "trivial" information among towns. That's why Hecate's Roman name is Trivia, a word that means "random facts." Many people find trivia fun and interesting. Modern examples of trivia games include Trivial Pursuit and *Jeopardy*.

According to Greek myth, Hecate helped

Demeter rescue Persephone, who went missing in the Underworld. Hecate is often pictured holding torches to light their way out. Her sacred animals include a dog and a polecat (similar to a ferret). When dogs howled at night, ancient Greeks believed that Hecate might be wandering the Earth with ghosts. **Melinoe** (mell-ee-NO or mell-ee-NO-ee) was a less important daemon, with many of the same traits as Hecate.